Jane Yolen is the author of ove[...] [...]ds, and adults. Winner of the World Fa[...] [...]ollection *Favorite Folktales from Around the World,* she has authored a dozen other folklore collections, including *Gray Heroes, Mirror, Mirror, Not One Damsel in Distress,* and *The Fairies' Ring.* Her work has won the Nebula Award, the Caldecott Medal, three Mythopoeic Society Awards, the Jewish Book Award, five bodies of work awards, and been nominated for the National Book Award. She lives in Massachusetts and St. Andrews, Scotland.

Among **Shulamith Oppenheim**'s many books are two fantasies, *The Selchie's Seed* and, for adults, *The World Invisible. Iblis,* the retelling of the Islamic version of the *Fall from Eden,* was an ALA Notable for older children, 1994. She lives in western Massachusetts.

Paul Hoffman is an illustrator who makes his home in Greenfield, Massachusetts. He began working as an illustrator for the University of Chicago, drawing ancient inscriptions in Luxor, Egypt. His work has appeared in the *New York Times* and he has illustrated several books published by Random House and St. Martin's Press.

The Fish Prince

and Other Stories
Mermen Folk Tales

by Jane Yolen
and Shulamith Oppenheim

illustrations by Paul Hoffman

Interlink Books
An imprint of Interlink Publishing Group, Inc.
New York • Northampton

For David and Felix, with love
—J. Y. and S.O.

First published in 2001 by

INTERLINK BOOKS
An imprint of Interlink Publishing Group, Inc.
99 Seventh Avenue • Brooklyn, New York 11215 and
46 Crosby Street • Northampton, Massachusetts 01060
www.interlinkbooks.com

Library of Congress Cataloging-in-Publication Data

Yolen, Jane.
The fish prince and other stories : mermen folk tales / Jane Yolen and Shulamith
Oppenheim.
    p. cm.
Includes bibliographical references and index.
    ISBN 1-56656-389-5 (hardcover) -- ISBN 1-56656-390-9 (pbk.)
1. Mermen. 2. Tales. I. Oppenheim, Shulamith Levey. II. Title.
GR910 .Y65 2001
398.21--dc21

                                                                    2001000996

Printed and bound in Canada

~

Mermen weep their pearly tears down a moon-green sea,
Blue fields are breathing their jade to the sun...
And a moment that ought to have lasted forever
Has come and gone before I knew.

—a poem of Tang Dynasty, 629–906

Contents

Prologue

It was in the sea that life began. For eons, single cell creatures moved blindly about in a vast playground of salt water. Then, by some miraculous push, a form was born. And for eons more, the oceans, lakes, rivers, streams, and ponds teemed with multi-celled life.

The miracle continued. Another thrust, another change, another twist, another transfiguration, and with a kind of random single-mindedness one creature pulled itself up onto a mud bank. Earthbound—but not quite.

For eons again, this new creature and its progeny lived between land and water, beneath the water or deep in primal ooze or surfacing for sun and air. The inheritors of this genetic mantle exist today: frog, salamander, toad, newt.

Others, journeying farther from their original watery home, became inexorably bound to mountain, tree, desert, sky. And then there were the few who, though earthbound for uncounted time, recapitulated the ancient story in reverse and found a haven back in the sea so that now they, too, live part-time beneath the water: walrus, sea lion, seal.

This, then, is humankind's heritage—sea and earth, earth and sea. Each conception sees the tale retold. A child in its mother's womb passes through the same mysterious stages that life-forms themselves passed through on their original journey. Suspended swimming in its amniotic fluid, the fetus at first develops gill slits and a tail. Perhaps it makes even more subtle passages as yet uncharted in that maternal sea. These stigmata appear, disappear, develop into something else, as the species' choice is re-established once again.

We are land's kind, now; earth-living, rooted in the soil. Yet the passage of our ancestors, like tribal markings, appear on our unborn selves, a reminder of a time when humans were something else.

Once the human child is born, these links with the past seem broken.

But not quite.

The first remaining link is physical. The human body is about seven-tenths water. The plasma, the clear liquid of the blood, bears a startling resemblance to sea water. In our veins flow a reminder of our first home; the veins themselves like old meandering rivers, branch and twist, a watery map beneath the skin.

The second link exists in the human imagination. We are myth-making creatures. Is it any wonder that many of our earlier myths revolve around the half-human, half-fish creatures who moved elegantly between two worlds? Drawn ever and ever back to their heritage sea, our ancestors created mermen partially in their own images.

Mer-*men*?

But surely this half-human, half-fish construct was female, an exotic siren languishing on a flat rock with green-gold hair, a scaly tail, smooth shoulders, and breasts as small and firm as bubble shells. Surely this mer creature, who rose seductively by the ship's prow, invitation unmistakable, was female.

No, indeed. Long before mermaids emerged to people our inner seas, long before they established their restless, inviting niche in human fantasy, another branch on the Fatal Woman tree of myth, there was the merman.

Born of the human need to dominate the great fruitful oceans, born of the human drive to control the vast destructive seas, born of the human desire to regulate the healing rains, born of the human wish to understand the tidal fluctuations, the merman emerged.

The merman was water personified. The imposing water gods could be wheedled, cozened, implored but—in the end—they were never fooled. How often were Poseidon or Neptune, Lir, Njord, and the rest pictured riding the waves, those "horses of the sea," along inhospitable shores, shaking their magical tridents or spears or cauldrons or fists at the weak, imploring humans on land? The sea gods called up storms or quieted waves. They flooded the lands. They gave the fisherfolk good harvests or small catches. They drowned the unwary.

Yet despite the importance of early fish-tailed gods such as Ea-Enki, Dagon, and others; despite the preponderance of mermen in the mythologies of Babylon, Greece, the British Isles, the Scandinavian peninsula, Germany; despite the mermen ranging along the Slavic shores and inland seas; despite the mermen found in Chinese and Japanese lakes, along the Polynesian island coasts, in the literature and lore of the Middle East, the merman might be called Legend's Forgotten Man. In the *Standard Dictionary of Folklore*, the section on mermaids is four times as long as that on mermen.

The reasons are not hard to find. Nature is most often considered female. Mother Nature. Mother Earth. The fecund earth goddess reigns in almost every culture. La Mer, the mother sea. "The sea lulls, water soothes, a woman comforts," say the old saws. The sea and water itself became a reflection of man's vision of the feminine element: soothing, yet treacherous. Furthermore, fishermen and sailors spending long months away from their wives and sweethearts fantasized sea women beckoning to them from the waves. Privation stimulates the imagination. Romance is born.

And so mermaids have gained notoriety while mermen are all but forgotten, weeping their pearly tears down a moon-green sea.

Yet mermen were there first, ruling over the Mother Sea as fish-tailed gods, swimming along untidy river bottoms, coasting on the tops of waves, or shapeshifting at will like Proteus among his seals.

They were there first and it is unnatural to leave them unremembered.

Our purpose here is to resurrect them, to reconstruct their unnatural histories. And who knows—the ocean is many fathoms deep. No human has seen it all. Perhaps a miracle waits in those uncharted depths, a miracle with a man's face, a broad chest, and the sinuous tail of a great fish. The merman may indeed live on, below the waves where he belongs and where—surely—he reigns.

Introduction

WHAT IS A MERMAN?

The great sea gods—Ea-Enki, Poseidon, Neptune, Kianda, Njord—are strictly mythological constructs. They were the rationale for every storm at sea, every benevolent wave. They explained the tidal patterns, the origin of fishes.

The rationale for the mermen, however, seem to be as various as the stories themselves.

Some mermen are remnants of river gods or gods of streams, fountains, wells, an extension of the myth-making that had created the mighty ocean gods.

Some mermen are remnants of ghostly tales, bugaboos used to frighten children into acceptable behavior. *Do not go by the banks of that swift stream or...*

Some mermen are explanations for accidental drownings. Some are folk memory of sacrificial rites.

Some mermen are misty bits of history, such as the Berber pirates who painted themselves blue and raided the northern shores of Europe, becoming the legendary Bluemen of the Minch.

Some mermen are deliberate lies, fabrications passed off on an unsuspecting audience, such as the monkey-fish mermen stitched together by enterprising Malaysians and sold to young English seamen in Victorian times.

Some mermen are misunderstood zoology, as when sailors long at sea spied a manatee, dugong, walrus, or seal and thought them merfolk.

Some mermen are simply boys or men with multiple birth defects—webbing between the fingers or toes, scaly skin, even the remnants of a tail. Possibly some are autistic as well, for recent studies have shown that autistic children, while not speaking, love to swim.

And some mermen are simply inexplicable. As one Dutch natural historian wrote, early in the eighteenth century:

> ... in the year 1652 or 1653, a lieutenant in the service of the [East India] Company saw two of these [mermen] in the gulf, near the village of Hennetelo, in the administrative district of Amboina. They were swimming side by side, which made him presume that one was male, the other female. Six weeks after, they reappeared in the same spot, and were seen by more than fifty persons. These monsters were of a greenish gray colour, from head to waist, with arms and hands, but their bodies tapered away...

If any narrative in the world deserves credit, it is this, for the merfolk were seen by so many witnesses. But was the sighting a hoax? A misunderstanding of native ceremony? A misreading of animal behavior? Or was it a true encounter with real mermen? Without scientific evidence, we can not know.

And what of the merman who sailors supposedly captured swimming off Spain. They reported he told them he was from Lierjanes and when they returned him there, he further revealed his name, which was Francisco de la Vega. Their description is neither fanciful nor overwrought. He had, they said, red hair, vacant eyes, fatty colorless flesh, and scales. Refusing to tell his captors any more about himself, they relaxed their guard, whereupon he escaped with his family into the sea.

•••

It is always possible—if highly improbable—that mermen did exist and exist no more. Perhaps like the passenger pigeon, the dodo, and the saber-toothed tiger, the merman is extinct.

Or perhaps, like the coelacanth, the merman is still waiting to be discovered by modern science. Perhaps he is even lounging on his coral bed right now, fingering a rosary of cowries, ready to rise on a midnight tide to tell his tale to the hitherto unbelieving world.

For most of us are non-believers in this particular myth. From early on, the disbelief has been palpable. This is from the French *Journal Encylopedique*, October 1764, in an article titled "Observations on Mermen."

Many people still believe fabulous tales. But in truth, it is humiliating to think that a part of the only "reasoning" beings that exist in nature should be made to live in a society with fish! If the existence of this type of "man" is admitted to and demonstrated, what difficulties and consequences (overwhelming) will fall upon terrestrial men! Because if this "animal" conforms exactly to ourselves, if it is organized in the same way, it must have ideas. They think, they reason, and we do not have an instinct finer than theirs. And these creatures give birth! Their women, it is said, resemble ours. As mothers, they are even tenderer than our European women! But the great question is: Do they have a soul! And if so, what good is it to have put a soul into the body of something destined to live and die with the fishes?

Chapter 1

MERMEN OF THE NORTHERN WATERS

Around the northern waters many stories of merfolk abound. But while today there are still stories about mermaids in the folk cultures, of the mermen scarcely a word is spoken. They did not often rise to meet mortals in the stories we have of them. And when they surfaced, unlike their mates, they were often ugly and ill-tempered.

It is a Swedish belief that, when the old pagan gods were defeated by Christianity, they took refuge in lakes, rivers, and streams. There they became merfolk. So sacrifices at river crossings, fords, bridges reflected these long-held heathen beliefs. Animals such as white horses, bulls, lambs were the usual sacrifice, but humans were not an unheard-of price for a safe crossing. Often in merman tales humans are drowned: folk memory at work in its elliptical way, remembering the old custom of sacrifice, disguising it in a more palatable way for modern retellings.

In northern waters mermen appeared in more than the folk and fairy tales. They were also identified in natural histories, listed as a separate species. There exists in one such, a folio of eight pages concerning *Genus merman*.

In sixteenth-century Norway it was said that a monk-fish had been captured by sailors. A short while later, a bishop-fish was hauled in. Supposedly it stood upright, wore a bishop's habit, but was covered with scales. Over fifty years later, in 1597, a "Negro fish"—a fish with the head of a black man— was discovered in the Northern waters.

These were not even unusual reports. Through the centuries such stories were repeated over and over, with small variations as to time and setting. Repeat a story enough and it will soon have the ring of truth.

Neckham reported in the twelfth century seeing a man-fish. In 1554 Rondeletius reported another. In 1663 sworn testimony was taken from sailors who said they had "captured a merman" who had been swimming off the Dutch coast and was caught by a lieutenant in the navy.

In 1726, a Dutch colonial captain wrote *A Natural History of Amboina*, in which he cited as fact in the section on fish "Zee Menschen" (sea men) and "Zee Wyven" (sea wives).

Why did such stories keep recurring? Medieval folk believed that everything on land had its counterpart in the sea. Many of the scientists of the time believed this, too.

Nix

These German river folk favored certain pools and streams where they lived in marvelous underwater palaces, sometimes with their own cattle grazing nearby. Their chosen rivers were the Saale, the Danube, and the Elbe.

The nix women, called nixies, were fish-tailed and beautiful. The men were ugly. Bearded, with sharp green teeth, green hair, and a fish tail, the nix men were thought to keep the souls of drowned land folk in upside-down pots. In fact, the Germans believed that drowning humans was a nix's main occupation. They said of the drowned, "The nix has drawn them to him." And since the nix demanded a yearly victim, the pall of human sacrifice hangs heavily over many a nix tale.

Happily, sacrifices other than human could appease certain Nix. In the Diemel river, for example, believers used to throw bread and fruit into the water once a year. Sailors also thought that a knife or nail in the bottom of their boats would have power to ward off the nix. As in much European fairy lore, cold iron is a powerful deterrent.

Occasionally, rather than drown a beautiful sacrifice, the nix would woo her. If the girl bore his child and the child was slow to obey the nix's call, the river would spurt a jet of blood. This was not only a sure sign of the nix's displeasure, it often meant that the child was actually dead. But if the nix was pleased or willing to forgive his child's misdeeds, a jet of pure white milk would rise up from the middle of the river. If indeed a nix married a human girl, he would also capture to serve as midwife. If she remained discreet about who her employer was, she would end up extremely well paid.

The main difference between the nix and humans was not their form or that one lived on land, the other in the water. To medieval storytellers, the important difference was that the nix had no soul. According to priests, the nix drowned humans to steal their souls.

THE NIX'S SOUL
Germany

It was a gray day, the sky overhead the color of old pearl. Klaus and Hans were playing by the riverside. They tossed stones into the water and tried to slip the flat ones along the tops of the waves.

Tiring of this game, the two boys strolled farther along the riverbank.

"I hear music," said Klaus.

Hans turned his head to listen. "Yes," he said at last. "A harp."

They ran toward the sound and when they came to a bend in the river, they saw a man sitting on a big black rock playing on a golden harp. Water rained down from his black hair and beard. When he opened his mouth and began to sing a psalm, the boys saw he had green teeth, long and pointed.

That was when they knew who the man was.

"A nix!" cried Hans. "He will drown us if he sees us. We must hurry away."

"No, he shall not hurt us," Klaus said. "For we are good Christians." He poked his brother on the arm. "Watch this."

Klaus turned toward the river and cupped his hands, calling out, "Why do you sing a psalm, nix? You know you will never be saved."

Hans turned pale and grabbed his brother's arm. "What are you doing? Now he will be furious with us. We will be drowned for sure."

But at Klaus' words, the nix threw his harp into the water where it sank without a sound. He put a scaly arm across his eyes and gave one sharp cry. Then he stood, flung himself into the water, and followed the harp into the deep.

Frightened, Hans took his brother's hand and pulled him toward home.

As they passed the church, Hans cried out, "Father Karl, Father Karl, Klaus has shamed a nix. He told the creature he would never be saved. Then the nix cried out and threw himself into the water."

Father Karl came out of the church quickly, and shook his head. "Ah, my poor boys, it is not the nix who is shamed but yourselves. You have sinned against the poor creature, reminding him of his lot. Go back and comfort him. Tell him that perhaps he may be saved. For none of God's creatures must be without hope."

Heads down, the boys returned to the riverbank and when they got around the bend, there was the nix once again sitting on his rock. This time he was not playing on his harp, but instead was weeping bitterly. The water raining down from his hair and beard could not match the flow from his eyes.

Hans felt deep shame, then. "What Father Karl said is true. No one without a soul could weep so bitterly."

Cupping his hands to his mouth, Klaus called, "Do not cry, nix. Our priest says that your redeemer liveth, too."

At that, the nix looked up and smiled his green smile, which was both terrible and beautiful to see. He put out his hand, and the little boys shivered. But the nix was not reaching toward them but toward the water.

Suddenly the golden harp burst through the surface and sprang into the nix's hand. He pulled the instrument to his chest and began to play joyfully. He played hymn after hymn while the two boys stood spellbound.

When finally the sun—bronze as an old penny—began to set, the nix flung his harp back into the river. Then he stood slowly and waved once at the boys, who stirred as if in a dream. Then he dove joyfully into the water and did not come up again.

∾

A version of this story is also told of the Swedish nekk, and can be found all over the Scandinavian countryside. Another popular version has the priest saying to a nekk, "Sooner will this cane that I hold in my hand grow green flowers than thou shalt attain salvation," at which point the cane bursts into flower. A less agreeable variant is found in Denmark where the creatures are not mermen but dwarves who, upon hearing they cannot be saved, turn the entire hillside to fire.

Nickelman or Nick

A black man above the waist, a fish below, the nickelman had extremely sharp teeth and his usual food was fish, but he also ate human children whom he snapped up and crushed with his fangs.

Every year in Thale a black cock was thrown into the river Bode to appease the nickelman. Even today in Ilseburg you can still buy little black figures in wooden boxes that spring up when the boxes are open.

BROTHER NICKEL
Germany/Grimm's

On the Isle of Rugen, in a thick forest, sits a deep, cloudy lake. Though the lake is rich with fish, the local people feared fishing there.

Many years ago some fishermen tried to fish there, put their boat in the water, then went home for their nets. When they returned, the boat was gone. They looked around for a long time, and at last found it stuck in the top of a tall beech tree.

"Who the devil put my boat up there?" cried one man.

A voice from the water called back, "The devils did not do anything. I did it with my brother Nickel."

~

Many other Teutonic and Norse countries have their own version of the Nix: Necker in the Netherlands; Neck in Norway; Nakk in Estonia; Nakki in Finland; Nokke in Denmark; Näk in Sweden.

Though these creatures are all related, each country of the northern waters has its own unique stories and versions of these mermen.

Necker
Necker women, like their German counterparts, sang beautifully. On land they could dance with a light, quick foot.

But the Necker men were to be feared. They sucked the blood of the drowned and even lured humans into the water to satisfy this thirst. Sometimes they cried in the night in the voice of a small, weeping child, thus enticing unsuspecting victims into the river.

One or two stories, though, tell of more pitiable necker men. Near Ghent, an old man was seen floating on the River Scheldt. Moaning and groaning, the old man frightened two children who ran from him. This caused him to cry even louder. When the children returned and asked him the cause of his distress, the necker sighed deeply and disappeared beneath the water.

Neck

The Norse neck or river spirit sometimes appeared as a boy with golden ringlets and a red cap. (Mermen and fairie creatures of other countries also were supposed to wear red caps.) Sometimes the neck played on the water's surface as a handsome young man, hiding his horse hoofs and tail. Perhaps in this incarnation he is related to the Scottish water kelpie, a shapeshifter who was sometimes human and sometimes horse. Most often, though, the neck appeared as an old man who sat on the cliff's edge and wrung his long beard till water flowed from it.

The neck was an emotional sort. He could become extremely angry upon finding out that a maiden had been unfair to her lover. In his righteous anger, he had been known to drown the pretty trifler. But, should the neck himself fall in love with a human girl, he was the most ardent and polite lover any maiden could wish for.

He was also famous for his ability to play upon a harp of gold. A human who wanted to play as well as a neck had to be willing to offer up two items for lessons: a black lamb and the offer of resurrection and redemption. The black lamb, of course, harkens back to the riverbank sacrifices from pre-Christian times. The second—the hope of redemption—is certainly an add-on from the days when the priests were trying to rid the countryside of heathenish practices.

In fact, the name "Neck/Nix/Nick" is the same as one of the names for the Devil: Old Nick. Though in some Norse and German dialects the word *nikr* means hippopotamus. Or water horse.

If a person was bothered by a neck, metal could be used to ward him off, particularly objects made of steel. As the country folk used to say, "Steel binds the neck."

There is a charm in Norway that goes:

Neck, neck, nail in the water!
The Virgin Mary casteth steel in the water!
Do you sink, I flit!

Nokken
The Norwegian merman was fish-tailed and had the ability to see into the future. This meant that for friends, the nokken gave warnings about impending disasters; for their enemies they kept silent.

THE GRATEFUL MERMAN
Norway

A crew from Nesna was fishing in Lofoten. One day while they were hauling in their nets, they caught sight of a man swimming near one of the boats' bows.

"Huttetu! I'm freezing!" the man cried.

A fisherman in that boat leaned over the side, pulled off a mitten, and threw it to the stranger.

The man in the water took the mitten, grinned, and sank back down into the sea. He did not come up again.

No one in the fishing boat spoke of what had happened, though they knew the man must have been one of the nokken. But to speak of it might have brought them into danger. Fishermen do not court the uncanny. They have enough danger without adding more. So they simply finished hauling in their nets and rowed toward land.

Finishing their evening chores, the men climbed out of their outer clothes and snuggled into their bunks. Soon they were all snoring. All, that is, except the one who had thrown his mitten overboard.

Suddenly by his bedside there was a strange, dark shadow leaning over him: the merman.

"Hey there, Mitten-man," cried the shadow, "there's lightning to the north and thunder in the sea!"

Mitten-man was suddenly wide awake. He sat up in his bunk, remembering that he and his mates had not bothered to draw their boats up onto the shore. It had been such fine weather when they'd come home, they hadn't thought it necessary.

Quickly he woke his companions and they dressed and dragged the boats way up on land, tying them fast.

As soon as they finished, the storm broke over them. Many another fisherman along the coast had his boat destroyed that day, by the great unpredictable storm. But not those warned by the grateful merman.

~

The freshwater nokken was considered a dangerous and cunning merman. So sure of his ability to capture and drown humans, he was often heard to call out, "The hour has struck but the man has not come."

On summer nights, it was said, the freshwater nokken would rise up from a lake in the shape of a white horse.

Sometimes the nokken waited for his victims in human form. In such a guise he would lure them onto the thin skin of ice over the lake, or convince them to ride with him in a leaky boat. Either way, once in the middle of the lake, the nokken would drag his victim down to the bottom.

Nokke

The Danish nokke appeared in several disguises. At times the nokke was a monster with a human head. Or at times a wild young boy with two long, shaggy golden curls and a red cap. At other times a handsome man with a dark beard wearing a cap as mossy green as his teeth.

When someone had drowned, it was said, "The nokke took him away."

Näkki

What distinguished the Finnish näkki from his cousins were his iron teeth and enormous size. He was hideous in the extreme.

In the western part of Finland, the näkki was thought to be half-human, half-beast, with horse's hoofs that propelled him under the water.

When shapeshifting, a näkki often became a human of such huge proportions, he could stand with one foot on the near shore of the sea and the other foot spanning the land to the farthest shore. Or he turned into a dog with a long beard, a buck wearing fishnet pouches between his horns, or a dog with an eye as big as a plate.

On the other hand the female of the species, the näkinneito, had a white and beautiful body, her hair curling over her shoulders to the small of her back. Her breasts were so huge, she could toss them over her shoulders. She was the only creature in the world who could love a näkki.

Näkk

The Estonians called their male water spirit a näkk. They lived down at the bottom of every river in the deepest spot. Anyone who drowned became a näkk. Often a human drowned by listening to the beautiful singing of a näkk and not paying attention to how close the waters were.

The female was called a nakineiu or nakineitsi. Fish-tailed and beautiful, she tended her long hair with a golden comb. But the male was an ugly monster with a cavernous mouth full of fish teeth, and he was quite capable of swallowing a human whole. His one saving grace was that when he opened that awful mouth to sing, the beauty of the song enchanted all who heard it.

The näkk of Estonia did not drown victims. Rather they warned of drowning. But they did devour any humans they caught. The näkk's favorite disguises were as men, children, and horses.

Fishermen on the Isle of Mohn developed a strange practice, a ritual to satisfy the näkk. Before setting out to sea, they would find a stone that fit comfortably in the hand. Spitting on the stone, the fishermen would fling it into the sea, calling out: "A cake to the näkk!" This was to satisfy the näkk's awful hunger.

THE MAIDEN AND THE NÄKK
Estonia

One time, long ago, a simple girl was walking along the seaside and she came upon a pretty boy who was wearing a handsome belt, the kind some well-off peasant might wear— all leather, with a leather tie instead of a buckle.

Covering his mouth with one hand, the boy begged sweetly, "Maiden, will you scratch my head for me. I have the most awful itch." Then he sang a little song that quite enchanted her.

So she did as he asked, and while she was so engaged, he fastened her to him by means of the belt. But as she continued to rub his head, he fell asleep.

Meanwhile, an older, wiser woman passed by and saw the two of them there. Recognizing the girl, and knowing her to be somewhat simple, the woman asked, "What are you doing?"

The girl explained and as she did so, freed herself from the belt.

The boy, however, slept sounder than before, his mouth wide open.

Seeing that, the woman grabbed the girl, crying, "Ha! That's no boy. See his fish teeth? He is a näkk! When he awakes, girl, he plans to have you for supper."

They ran down the road a ways and when they turned to look back, the näkk had vanished.

~

Belief in the nix and their counterparts in the northern waters was once so common that plants and stones were named after them. Today, though the belief in water spirits is reflected only in stories and tales, the names remain: *Nixblume* (a German flower), *Nackblad* (a Swedish flower), *Nokkeblomster* (a Danish flower), *Nakora* (Nix's ear, a Swedish shellfish), and *Nackbrod* (Nack's bread, a Swedish stone).

Fossegrimen

The spirits living in Norwegian waterfalls were called fossegrimen. (*Fos* is Norwegian for "falls.") Of all the underwater folk, they were the finest musicians. While the nix and his cousins claimed to be the best harp players, the fossegrim was master of the fiddle.

Anyone wishing to learn fiddle-playing from the fossegrim had to bring a black lamb or a white goat on a calm, dark evening and throw it into the falls so that it landed northward. A plump joint of meat at the widest part of the falls was also acceptable.

But humans had to beware! The fossegrimen were very particular. If the lamb was not black enough or the evening not dark enough or the joint not plump enough, the merman would not come out to give the lessons. And if the goat was too lean, the joint too stringy, the fossegrim would only teach his pupil how to tune—and nothing more.

However if all was satisfactory, the young and handsome fossegrim came to the edge of the falls. To the edge—but never entirely out of the water. He then held his pupil's right hand on the fiddle strings, guiding it up and down until blood started from the fingertips. And then the pupil was able to play until trees danced and the torrents in the waterfall stood still.

It is said that one can always tell which fiddler has been taught by a fossegrim, for he fiddles backwards, fingering with his right hand and bowing with his left.

Strömkarl

In German, "strömkarl" means river sprite or river man. Like the Norwegian fossegrim, the strömkarl was a master musician whose tunes truly enchanted.

The most famous strömkarl tune was "Strömkarl's Lag." (Lag is a lay or a tune.) It had eleven variations, but only ten of them could be played by a mortal. The eleventh was reserved for an inhabitant of the faerie world. When it was played, tables and benches, cups and candles danced. Graybeards and grandmothers, the blind and the lame, even babies in their cradles leaped to their feet and whirled around. When the eleventh variation was played, charmed milk would spring from a maiden's breast.

Like the fossegrim, the strömkarl dwelled inside waterfalls. But he could also be found in a millpond, lingering by the mill wheel, and playing along to its melancholy whirring.

To propitiate the strömkarl, and to win music lessons, a would-be pupil had to sacrifice a black lamb on a Thursday evening. As with the fossegrim, if the sacrifice was poor, the pupil was only taught to tune the instrument. But if the sacrificial lamb was a good one, the strömkarl grabbed the pupil by the hand, twisting his right hand back and forth till the blood ran right out of the fingertips. After that, the pupil would be a master musician.

The strömkarl was not only German. He was a Norwegian and Swedish water spirit as well.

Havmand

The Danes tell of the havmand, a spirit of burn and spring. A handsome, green or black-bearded man, he was a friendly sort who could live either in the spring or on rocky cliffs overlooking the sea.

However his wife was to be avoided at all costs! Known as the havfrue, she was a nasty temptress who in the form of a beautiful, shivering woman sometimes lured fishermen from their homes.

The Danish havmand has been known to fall in love with a human woman, taking her for a wife. In the popular Danish ballad "Agnete og Havmanden," (Agnes and the Merman) the earthly maiden is carried away by her mer-lover:

Her ears he stopp'd and her mouth he stopp'd
And down to the bottom of the sea they dropped.

And the result of this union:

Eight years she dwelt with the merman there,
And under the sea seven children bare.

When Agnes pleads to go above to church, he begs her not to forget him or their children. But when she sits down and prays, all memory of her life below leaves her. The poor merman makes the trip into the church himself to confront her, begging her to think on the children waiting below. She answers:

I think not of the grown ones, nor yet of the small,
Of the babe in the cradle, I'll think least of all.

Versions of this ballad have been collected in Sweden, Norway, Germany, and Slovenia. It is so popular, it has its own motif number: C713. It formed the basis for Matthew Arnold's famous poem "The Forsaken Merman," which begins:

Come dear children, let us away;
Down and away below!
Now my brothers call from the bay,
Now the great winds shoreward blow,
Now the salt tides seaward flow,
Now the wild white horses play,
Champ and chafe and toss in the spray.

Children dear, let us away!
This way, this way!

and ends:

We will gaze, from the sand-hills,
At the white, sleeping town;
At the church on the hillside—
And then come back down.
Singing: "There dwells a loved one,
But cruel is she!
She left lonely for ever
The kings of the sea."

Three Danish sailors swore in affidavits that they had come upon a havmand only a mile off the coast of Denmark, near Landscrona. Assuming it was a dead body, they rowed speedily toward it. As they approached, the body sank, then surfaced again, and turned toward them. As the chronicler Pontippidan wrote:

He stood in the same place for seven or eight minutes and was seen above the water breast high. At last the sailors grew apprehensive of some danger and began to retire; upon which the monster blew up his cheeks and made a lowing noise and then dived from their view… He appeared like an old man, strong-limbed, with broad shoulders, but his arms they could not see. His head was small in proportion to his body, and had short curled black hair, which did not reach below his ears; his eyes lay deep in his head, and he had a meagre face with a black beard; about the body downwards, the merman was quite pointed like a fish.

Another "genuine" havmand was said to have been taken off the coast of Denmark and exhibited in London at the time of Queen Anne. The bill announcing its display read in part: "The whole creature is very large and weighed (according to the computation) at least Fifty Tons and is Seventy Feet in length. His upper part resembles a man, but from the middle downward is a fish." From the description, the creature sounds more like a walrus than anything else.

Soedroven

In Norway, the sailors and fisherfolk feared the soedroven, a headless old man. Such a sighting portended danger: storms, drownings, a wreck at sea.

Wasserman

The German wasserman (waterman) loved coming ashore to dance at parties with pretty girls. He could be easily recognized by his linen smock, which was always wet at the left side on the bottom, no matter how close to the fire he came nor how long he had danced. But as he was an excellent dancer, his partners never complained about the wet hem hitting them in the leg. However, they were careful not to let the wasserman walk them home after the dance for he was unreliable.

When a wasserman bought grain at the market, the farmers kept a careful eye on his purchases. If the wasserman paid above the market value for his grain, a poor growing season would follow and prices would rise. If he bargained, there would be an abundant harvest and prices would fall.

There was a dangerous side to the wasserman, too. The poet Spenser wrote:

> The griesly Wasserman, that makes his game
> The flying ships with swiftness to pursue.

Water-Smith

In Germany are a number of stories about a water-smith, who worked faster and with more accuracy than any other smith. Like the elves in the fairy tale "The Shoemaker and the Elves" he cannot be paid for his work, or he disappears.

THE BLACK FOREST WATER-SMITH
Germany/Grimm's

In Seewenweiher, deep in the Black Forest, was a lake in which a little water-smith lived. He would come out during the day and work long hours with the local people. They would set aside his breakfast and dinner. But at night he would go back to his lake.

He promised to work with them as long as they gave him not too much and not too little to do. But one day, one or another folk forgot the rule, and the little water-smith was angry.

To show him how much they were grateful to him, the people made him a new coat and presented it to him.

The little water-smith looked at them with sad deep green eyes. "When one is paid off," he said, "one must go away. I'll come no more."

They begged and pleaded, but it was no use. They never saw him again.

~

Draug
The Norwegian draug was a strange sea spirit who sailed about in half a boat. To see a draug meant mortal danger. In order to make it back to shore alive, a sailor who spied a draug had to row frantically in order to get back to land and safety before the draug caught up to him.

Icelandic Merman
The people of Iceland used to tell of a merman who was a dwarf with an enormous head and broad hands. To the waist he was a human, but below the waist a seal. He was also a herder of sea cows.

When an Icelander says, "And the merman laughed!" it refers to the mocking of foolish questions. The phrase comes from the following famous tale:

THE MERMAN LAUGHED
Iceland

There was a certain old farmer who went out fishing and caught a sea-dwarf in his net. The creature had a big head and broad, thick-knuckled hands like a human, but he was shaped like a seal from the navel down.

"Teach me your magic and I shall let you go," the farmer demanded.

But the merman shook his head. So the farmer took him ashore against his will.

Just as they arrived on shore, the farmer's young and lusty wife came down to the shore and greeted her husband, kissing and fondling him. The farmer was pleased and praised his wife outrageously. But when the farm dog came and leaped on him, trying to lick his face, the farmer drove the animal away with a fierce blow.

At that the merman laughed.

"Why do you laugh?" asked the farmer.

The merman shrugged his shoulders. "At stupidity," he said.

The farmer set out across his land, the merman flung over his shoulder, and he tripped over a tussock. Cursing the tussock heartily, the farmer cried out, "Why has such a useless hummock ever been sent by fate to stand on my land."

The merman laughed again, saying, "This farmer has no sense."

Gritting his teeth, the farmer carried the merman into his house where he kept the creature for three days.

Now during that time, some traveling merchants came by with wares to sell.

"Boots," said the farmer. "I have never been able to get boots with soles as thick and as strong as I would like. Have you any?"

The merchants insisted they had the finest quality boots.

So the farmer picked over the pairs of boots. "Na, na—this is too thin. That is too poorly made. They will all have holes in them in no time."

And the merman laughed. "Clever men make the biggest fools," he said as the merchants left.

Rounding on the merman, the farmer demanded that he explain himself.

"Not until you return me to the sea," the merman said. "Right back to the very fishing bank where you pulled me out."

The farmer cocked his head to one side and the merman continued.

"If you do that," said the merman, his dark eyes shining, "I shall squat on the blade of your oar and answer all your questions. As you know, mermen cannot lie. But I will not say a word more lest you take me home."

After three days of silence from the creature, the farmer gave up. He gathered up the merman and hauled him back to the very fishing bank where he'd been caught.

The merman was as good as his word. He squatted on the oar blade. "Ask away," he told the farmer.

"What gear should a fisherman use to get good catches?" asked the farmer.

The merman rolled his eyes. "Chewed and trodden iron for the hooks, the forging done where one can hear both river and wave. Then temper the hooks in the foam and sweat of tired horses. Use a fishing line made from a gray bull's sinews and cord from raw horsehide. For bait use birds' gizzards and flounders, but human flesh on the middle bight. The barb of a fishhook must point outwards."

The farmer took note of all the merman had to say.

"Ask on," said the merman. "I am certain you have more questions."

"That I do," said the fisherman. "It is about your laughter."

The merman smiled.

"Why did you laugh when I praised my wife and struck my dog?"

The merman smiled again. "I laughed at your stupidity, farmer. The dog loves you as dearly as his own life, but your wife wishes you were dead and is a whore."

The fisherman looked pained at that. "And why did you laugh when I cursed the tussock?"

"Because it covers a treasure destined for you. There's plenty of money beneath it."

"And when I could not find the boots I so sorely needed, why did you laugh yet again?"

The merman smiled a third time. "Those boots you wear now will last you the rest of your life, farmer. For you have but three more days to live." And with that, the merman plunged off the oar blade and into the sea.

And in time everything the merman said proved to be true.

The earliest mermen in Icelandic written literature are found in *Helf's Saga*. When the hero Helf and his men come upon a merman, they keep him on land for a spell, during which time he sings this:

Cold fish to the eyes!
Flesh raw to the teeth,
A shroud to the dead!

Flit me back to the sea!
Henceforth never
Men in ships sailing!
Draw me to dry land
From the depths of the sea!

Other merman are in the Icelandic Doomsday Book, *Landnama*, which includes accounts of such creatures discovered off the island of Grimsey in 1305 and 1329.

But perhaps the most exciting description of an Icelandic merman came from a priest serving in that country several centuries ago. The account concerns the remains of a merman found in the belly of a shark captured off the northwest coast of Iceland:

> The lower part of the animal was entirely eaten away, whilst the upper part, from the epigastric and hypogastric region, was in some places partially eaten away, in others completely devoured. The sternum, or breastbone, was perfect. This animal appeared to be about the size of a boy eight or nine years old, and its head was formed like that of a man. The anterior surface of the occiput was very protuberant, and the nape of the neck had a considerable indentation, or sinking. The alae of the ears were very large, and extended a good way back. It had front teeth that were long and pointed, as were also the larger teeth. The eyes were lustreless, and resembled those of a codfish. It had on its head long, black, coarse hair, very similar to the *fucus filifornis*, this hair hung over the shoulders. Its forehead was large and round. The skin above the eyelids was much wrinkled, scanty, and of a bright olive color, which was indeed the hue of the whole body. The chin was cloven, the shoulders were high, and the neck uncommonly short. The arms were of their natural size, and each hand had a thumb and four fingers covered with flesh. Its breast was formed exactly like that of a man, and there was also to be seen something like nipples; the back was also like that of a man. It had very cartilaginous ribs; and in parts where

the skin had been rubbed off, a black, coarse flesh was perceptible, very similar to that of a seal.

Dracae

Germanic water spirits of the Rhone Valley, these creatures used to entice woman into the streams where they were washing by floating in the form of golden cups. The earliest written instance of this legend can be found in Gervaise of Tilbury's manuscript as part of the *Otia Imperialia*, written in 1211. It is also the earliest reported version of the tale type #4050, "The hour has come, but not the man." (*See* Nokken, page 10.)

Cacce-olmai

This waterman of Lapland was a god of fishing, directing the fish to nets and lines. Laplanders used to put an image of the Cacce-olmai in a crevice by the stream to keep themselves from harm and also to bring themselves luck.

The Russian Laplanders once believed in a similar being, the Cacce-jielle, a dangerous creature who dragged unwary humans under the sea. A shapeshifter, the Cacce-jielle could become an old man, a naked child, or a fish. Seeing him was a portent of disaster. But the Cacce-jielle could be propitiated by sacrifices of corn, bread, and brandy.

Ravgga

Another Lapland merman, this one lived under the water in human shape. He knew ahead of time which tempests would occur, what shipwrecks and drownings would happen. If a ravgga was seen checking out boat accessories, there is no doubt a passenger in that craft would drown. However, if a human on the boat walked around the ravgga with a bit of firesteel, the merman would be forced to give up the name of the future victim and the time of his fate.

Nykur or Nennir

This water horse was believed to roam Iceland as well as the Faroes, a string of eighteen islands between Norway and Iceland. He looked like a horse, but all his hoofs were backwards. The nykur liked to drown people by enticing them onto his back. If, however, he heard himself named, the nykur lost his power.

Some nykurs could also assume human form, sitting on rocks and grooming themselves with golden combs. One such was said to have been enchanted by a priest who threw a rock at him, crying, "Now you shall go into the stone." That stone, say the Faroese, can still be seen on Lakeside Slope near Leitis Water, and is called "The Gravestone."

Like the kelpies of Scotland, the nykur was also used occasionally to haul stones.

THE NYKUR OF LEITIS WATER
Faroe Islands

One evening five brothers went over to Leitis Water to play. While they were on the strand, a great black horse came out of the water, shook himself all over, and stood nearby. He whickered softly.

"Let's get a ride," cried Nika, the oldest brother, and they all piled on, except for the youngest, who was too small to get up on his own.

As soon as the four were mounted, the horse headed toward the lake. The littlest boy still wanted a ride and he called after them, "Brother Nika, wait for me."

Only he was so little, he could barely speak properly, and it came out "Brudder Nykur."

Thinking the child had said his name, the nykur lost all his power and the brothers were saved.

∼

Klabautermann

This German ship-spirit was a funny little man no more than two or three feet tall. He had second sight and often dined with the ship's captain. While he was not strictly a merman (he didn't live under water) the klabautermann was occasionally taken for one, especially along the eastern Baltic coast.

The klabautermann entered a ship with the chips of wood used for the keel, and he lived there. With his red jacket, seaman's trousers, and ever-present pipe, he was a jolly spirit and not at all frightening. Good-hearted as well, he warned the ship's captain of trouble ahead. Or he would wake a sleeping helmsman with a slap.

The klabautermann also worked late at night caulking and repairing his ship, checking on cracks in the mast, and giving orders during a storm.

But should a klabautermann leave the ship during a voyage, following a line of rats, that ship was doomed. Shimmering for a single moment on the ocean waves, he disappeared. To the ocean bottom? To the shore? No one knows for sure.

A famous poem by Henry Wadsworth Longfellow tells about the Klabautermann. He takes some poetic license with the "facts" and uses an alternate spelling. Here is a section:

And one was spinning a sailor's yarn
About Klaboterman,
The Kobold of the sea; a spright
Invisible to mortal sight,
Who o'er the rigging ran.

Sometimes he hammered in the hold,
Sometimes upon the mast,
Sometimes abeam, sometimes abaft,
Or at the bows he sang and laughed,
And made all tight and fast.

He helped the sailors at their work,
And toiled with jovial din;
Helped them hoist and reef the sails,
He helped them stow the casks and bales,
And heave the anchor in.
But woe unto the lazy lout,
The idlers of the crew;
Them to torment was his delight,
And worry them by day and night,
And pinch them black and blue...

From a French missionary in the seventeenth century comes
the following account, found in *Journal Encylopedique*:

A Dutch captain by the name of Baker, in charge of a ship
named *The Swallow*, had the following experience. Onto the
deck of the ship, in the midst of busy sailors, jumped a
merman. Their astonishment grew when they heard the
creature speaking Dutch and asking them for a pipe that he
might have a smoke! He was covered with scales and his hands
were joined like fish fins. His body ended in a tail. He looked
to be about thirty years old. Captain Baker asked him who he
was. "I am a Dutchman who sailed on a vessel when I was eight
years old. The vessel capsized with everything on it and in it.
Somehow I did not drown, but became as you see me today."
Looking at the captain, the merman had the feeling that he was
going to be seized, so he threw himself back into the sea. The
captain wrote up the incident and submitted it to the Admiral
in Amsterdam as soon as the ship arrived in port.

Chapter 2

MERMEN OF RUSSIA
AND THE SLAVIC COUNTRIES

Russia and its neighboring Slavic countries occupy a vast land mass. The northern coast stretches for thousands of miles along the Bering Sea and Arctic Ocean. A great headland projects eastward into part of the Arctic and the Pacific.

Russia is also the home of one of the longest rivers in the world—the Volga—as well as two inland seas, the Caspian and Black. Yet there are surprisingly few mermen stories for all that.

There are, however, a number of stories about water snakes that turn into men and marry human women.

Vodyani

This Slavic freshwater spirit lived in a crystal palace at the bottom of a lake or river. He was depicted as humanoid, with paws, horns, and a tail. Infrequently, he was also pictured as a huge man covered with grass or moss or as an old man with green hair and a green beard. His red eyes shone through the water, lighting up his long nose. That nose—said the Slavs— was as long as a fisherman's boot.

The vodyani never died. Instead they had a strange pattern of growth—aging with the waning of the moon, growing young as it waxed.

But new moon or old, the vodyani were wicked, treacherous creatures who captured humans by making great splashing sounds. The humans caught in this manner were drowned and taken to huge underwater palaces as slaves to the vodyani.

In olden days, a miller who had the ill fortune to find a vodyani in his millpond was forced to sacrifice a human child to appease the spirit. Either that, or lose his own life.

Vu-murt

Related to the vodyani was the vu-murt, the Man of the Waters, a Votjak water spirit known to the Finno-Ugric people in the district of Kazan.

The vu-murt waited naked in the water, combing his long black hair. The vu-murt, though, was actually afraid of humans, hiding in the water when one passed by. Still, if the proper sacrifice was given—such as a duck stuck down an ice hole—the vu-murt overcame his fears and gave aid to the human who asked for it: rain, fertility, health, and luck in fishing.

At times the vu-murt lay in the water disguised as a great pike fish. But he was easy to distinguish because he slept with his head in the opposite direction of all the other fish!

Some folklorists say that the vu-murt was able to change his sex, becoming a woman. Others that the female vu-murt is actually the vu-murt's mate and that twice a year the vu-murts held weddings below the water, causing ice to break up underfoot or giant waves to inundate the countryside.

Wodny Muz

The Polish waterman lived in the lakes and rivers with his wife, the wodna zona. He tempted passers-by to swim and then drowned them. A corpse drowned by a wodny muz could always be identified by the blue spots on its body.

The wodny muz often went into the marketplace dressed in a red cap and a linen jacket with a wet hem.

Morskoi Tsar

In Russian folklore, the Morskoi Tsar was the water king. His daughters were beautiful maidens known as rusulkas who appeared on the water as swans, geese, ducks, or spoonbills.

The Morskoi Tsar lived under the water in crystal halls of

great splendor. He left his palace only to search out human victims. Having daughters of his own, he also sought boys or princes, who inevitably carried off one of the daughters.

Another name for the water king was Chudo Morskoe, or water giant. In the stories about the water giant, it is he who falls in love with a human, carrying her off to his palace of crystal and light. To this day in Slovenia, when the rivers flood and the waters rumble and growl over stony beds, the country folk say, "It is the water giant walking on the water with his clogs."

An interesting note—the word for walrus in use among European sailors in the seventeenth century was "morse," and at least one scholar—Horace Beck in *Folklore and the Sea*—sees a possible connection with the Morskoi Tsar.

THE SEA KING AND VASILISA THE WISE
Russia

Once there was a king who was about to shoot an eagle. Three times the eagle stopped him, saying, "Do not shoot me. Some day I shall be useful to you."

So the king relented and took the eagle back to his palace.

The eagle ate and ate and ate some more till there was nothing left in the kingdom—cattle, grain, fruits, or fish.

Then the eagle said to the king, "Climb on my back."

So the king climbed upon the eagle's back and away they flew. But over the ocean three times the eagle dropped the king into the water and three times he plucked him from the waves.

"Now my king," said the eagle, "you know the fear of death, for I could see you were frightened. Frightened as I was when you were about to shoot me."

They flew on, passing over the houses of the eagle's two sisters, till the eagle said, "Now I will leave you, sire. But I give you a ship and two coffers, one green, one red. Do not open them until you are home. Open the red one in the back garden and the green in the front garden."

The king bade the eagle farewell and sailed to a certain island. On going ashore, his curiosity was so great, he opened the red coffer. Out came so much cattle of every kind, there was hardly any room for them all.

"How shall I gather this herd together?" the king wondered, when suddenly he beheld a man coming out of the water.

"I shall gather your herd together," said the sea man, "but on one condition. Give me that which you do not know is in your house."

The king thought: *I know everything in my house.* And so he agreed.

What should he learn on returning home? His wife had given birth to a son!

He wept as he fondled the child, fearing to tell his wife the truth, and besides he thought: *That seaman does not know where I live.* So he went out into the back garden and opened the red coffer, and out came cattle and sheep and goats beyond counting. Then he went into the front garden and opened the green coffer and there appeared flowers and fruits of every size and hue.

The king was in such rapture at the return of all the eagle had eaten—and more—that he forgot the promise he made to the seaman.

•••

Years passed. And one day the king was walking by the river. Suddenly out of the water came the same seaman, who told him, "You have forgotten your debt. Now you must pay."

What could the king do? He went back and told the queen and the prince the truth. Weeping, they took the prince down to the seashore and left him there.

But the prince wandered into a nearby forest and soon saw a hut in which lived Baba Yaga, the witch. He spoke to her politely, which was lucky. Otherwise she might have eaten him.

She smiled at the prince with her iron teeth. "Go back to the seashore, my son," she said. "There twelve spoonbills will turn into twelve lovely maidens bathing. Creep up and steal the shift of the eldest. Then go to the Sea King."

"Thank you, grandmother," said the prince, who was lucky. She still could have eaten him. Then he did as Baba Yaga instructed.

Of course the eldest maiden could not fly away without her shift. "Please return what you have taken," she said, "and I shall be useful to you."

He did so, but asked, "Pray tell me your name."

"Vasilisa the Wise," she said, put on her shift, turned into a spoonbill, and flew after her sisters into the setting sun.

•••

The prince set off to find the Sea King, wading deep and deeper into the water until at last he came to the Sea King's palace.

"I have been waiting for you for a long time, my friend," said the Sea King. "Build me a crystal bridge in one night, or else you will lose your head."

The prince sat out in the Sea King's palace and wept because he could not do any such thing. "Alas, my mother, alas my father," he cried, "I shall see you no more."

Along came Vasilisa. "Go to sleep. The morning is wiser than the evening."

She put him to sleep and when he was snoring, gave a mighty whistle. From everywhere came workmen and the bridge was completed before sunrise.

Then Vasilisa woke the prince, who was greatly relieved. She handed him a broom and he swept the bridge.

"Bravo!" said the Sea King. "But there is another task you must complete. I desire a garden by tomorrow—tall flowering trees with ripe fruit on their bows, and birds flying everywhere. Otherwise I will have your head."

•••

The prince sat out in the Sea King's palace and wept because he could not do any such thing. "Alas, my mother, alas my father," he cried, "I shall see you no more."

Along came Vasilisa. "Go to sleep. The morning is wiser than the evening."

She put him to sleep and when he was snoring, gave a mighty whistle. From everywhere came gardeners and by morning there was a garden to gladden the heart of any Sea King.

When the Sea King saw the garden, he embraced the prince. "Choose a bride from my twelve daughters. They are all alike. If you choose three times the same, she will be your wife. Otherwise I will have your head."

•••

Vasilisa learned of the trial and came to the prince. "Do not worry, my love. The first time I shall wave a handkerchief. The second time I shall adjust my dress. The third time a fly shall settle on my head."

So the twelve sisters came out, dressed alike in red dresses with white embroidery. Their headdresses were exactly the same as well. They were all tall and strong boned with eyes the color of the sea.

"Choose," said the king.

The prince looked carefully and one of the princesses waved a handkerchief. "That one," he said.

The Sea King nodded. "Again."

The twelve princesses shifted around and around and finally came to a halt. One of them pulled at the bodice of her dress.

"That one," said the prince.

The Sea King smiled again.

This time when the twelve princesses shifted around, the prince was turned as well. And when they had all stopped shifting, the prince looked carefully.

"No one is to move," said the Sea King.

All of the princesses stood still. But a little fly flew round and about one of the princesses and landed on her headdress.

"That one," said the prince.

So the prince and Vasilisa the Wise were married and after their fathers died, they ruled both sea and land for the rest of their days.

∼

THE SPEEDY MESSENGER
Russia

In a certain land, a poor peasant decided to clear a swamp that took years to pass through, for the road around it was circuitous and rutted. He set about the work with his three sons: Ivan, Vasily, and Semyon.

At last there lay a straight road for travelers and horsemen and all the streams were traversed by sturdy white hazelwood bridges.

"Go," the poor man said to his eldest son. "Go, Ivan, and hide under the first bridge and hear what the folk say of us."

So Ivan hid. Soon two hermits walked over the bridge saying, "To him who laid this bridge and cleared the road, whatever he asks of the Lord, the Lord will give him."

On hearing these words, Ivan came out of hiding and announced that he and his father and brothers were the bridge builders.

"What do you wish of the Lord?" asked the hermits.

"That I be rich for the rest of my life," said Ivan.

"Go, then," said the hermits, "into that field and find an ancient oak. Under that oak is a vault. In the vault is gold and silver and precious stones. They are yours."

And so it was.

•••

Next day the peasant sent his son Vasily who, on hearing the same words from the same hermits, made the announcement, wishing for enough bread till he die.

"Go," said the hermits, "and stake out this fresh piece of land. Plough it, sow it, reap it, and you shall never lack for bread."

And so it was.

•••

When it was Semyon's turn, he asked to serve as a soldier to the great tsar.

"Choose something else," suggested the hermits. "A soldier's life is hard and you will fall captive to the Sea King."

But Semyon insisted. "My masters, you said to choose and I have chosen."

"Then we give you our blessing," they said, and turned Semyon into a fleet-footed stag, a hare, and a little bird with a golden head, one right after the other.

"Now go, young Semyon," said the hermits. "Whenever you have need to be fast, you can turn yourself into one of these creatures for we have taught you how."

•••

So Semyon entered the tsar's service and he fought bravely.

Now one time the tsar was caught by his enemies without his special battle mace and sharp sword. "My daughter's hand in marriage to he who can speed home the fastest and bring these to me," he cried, "for I must go to battle in the morning."

Off went Semyon, first as a bird, then as a hare, at last as a great stag. He reached the palace and sought out the princess. "Your father desires his mace and sword," he cried, "for he must do battle in the morning."

The king's daughter was delighted with the speed of the handsome young messenger and she cut off a tuft of the stag's hair as proof of his magic. "Go fast, great stag," she whispered to him.

But as he was returning with the mace and sword, tiredness overcame Semyon and he lay down to rest on a beach, not a hundred paces from the king's camp. As he slept, one of the tsar's generals passed by and found him with the weapons at his side. Taking the weapons, the general pushed Semyon into the sea where the Sea King seized him and carried him to the deepest depths.

•••

For a year Semyon served the Sea King, weeping bitterly.

Then one day the Sea King said to him, "Well, Semyon, would you like to go back to see your world?"

"I would, sire," Semyon said.

So the Sea King carried him out at midnight and left him on the shore where he was bound by the night.

"Oh, Lord, give me some sun," prayed Semyon, for he knew that only sun could melt his bonds.

But the Sea King came again and snatched him back before daylight.

Once again Semyon was left weeping bitterly, but the Sea King asked again, "Would you like to go back to see your world?"

Semyon nodded. But again he was set onto the shore at night and snatched back by the Sea King before dawn.

When a third time the Sea King toyed with Semyon, putting him onto the shore at midnight, Semyon once more prayed. "Oh, Lord, give me some sun."

This time the sun shone immediately, though it was not yet dawn, and the bonds melted and the Sea King could not take him back.

Semyon set out for the tsar's palace and got there just as the princess was being married to the wicked general who had stolen the mace and sword from him.

"It was I, great tsar, as stag and hare and bird, who reached the princess and brought back the mace and sword. But one long year I have been forced to serve the Moskoi Tsar because the general threw me into the sea."

"There is no proof," cried the wicked general.

But the princess reached into her bodice and pulled out the tuft of stag hair. "Here, father, is proof of all Semyon says, for he came to collect your weapons as a stag."

The general was put to death at once and Semyon was married to the princess and made the tsar's heir.

And how do I know this? I was there, and threw my boot at the rat.

~

Vetehinen

In Russo-Finland lived the malignant "water dweller" who loved to drown humans. Occasionally, though, his presence signaled luck for fisherman. As with many creatures from the faerie world, the vetehinen were afraid of metal objects.

Kul

Sometimes known as *vasa*, the black, hairy, and very wet kul was a Suryan sea dweller. He sat upon the shore shaking himself like a great damp dog and combing his sea-green hair. If he sat by a mill, he grabbed hold of the mill wheel, causing damage to both the mill and the grain.

When the kul emerged from his underwater home, he left behind a wife and children. Making mischief was his business alone. That mischief consisted of throwing himself from the water to the shore, causing great waves to rise up and foam. Or he wandered through the countryside slapping the clean wash on lines with his wet, hairy hands. Or on shore in the middle of the night, he howled long and hideously, waking the neighborhood.

Master of the Waters

The Samoyed—a Siberian Mongolian people scattered along the Arctic coast of the Ural area—used to tell of this merman, a dangerous carrier of disease.

In the old days, if illness struck a Samoyed family, they

would hang the clothes of the stricken one near the river for the Master of the Waters to find in place of the intended victim.

The Samoyeds also used to put money at the mouth of the river as a sacrifice to the Master in the hopes of good fishing.

Vit-khan

This water spirit of the Vogul, a people from the Ural Mountains, also insisted on sacrifices. He had a daughter who liked to marry humans.

Chebeldei

Siberian tribes once believed in many water spirits. Almost all were malignant and male creatures, lurking just below the surface of rivers, lakes, and marshes.

The sole intent of such spirits was to drown humans. The most repulsive of these—the chebeldei—had noses eighteen meters long.

Abaasy

Siberian watermen, these mermen had seven iron teeth each, as well as iron hair and eyelashes. Of an ardent nature, they stole human women in order to marry them.

Finally here are two stories from history rather than folklore. The first concerns two mermen captured in the Baltic Sea.

The sailors presented the two mermen to the King of Poland in 1531, according to the historian Gisbertus Germannus. One of them was a bishop-fish. Unhappy being taken from the sea, the bishop-fish pleaded for his life, using signs that a clergyman interpreted for the king. The bishop-fish's eloquence moved the king to have both the fish-men returned to the sea in—as Germannus says—"a reverential and dignified manner."

The second concerns a certain Captain Weddell, well known for his explorations around the South Pole. He recorded in his journal:

A boat's crew were employed on Hall's Island, when one of the crew, left to take care of some produce, saw an animal whose voice was ever musical. The sailor had lain down, and about ten o'clock he heard a noise resembling human cries; and as daylight in those latitudes never disappears at this season, he rose and looked around, but on seeing no person, returned to bed. Presently, he heard the noise again, rose a second time, but still saw nothing. Conceiving, however, the possibility of a boat being upset, and that some of the crew might be clinging to some detached rocks, he walked along the beach a few steps, and heard the noise more distinctly, but in a musical strain. Upon searching around, he saw an object lying on a rock a dozen yards away from the shore, at which he was somewhat frightened. The face and shoulders appeared of human form, and of a reddish color; over the shoulders hung long green hair; the tail resembled that of a seal, but the extremities of the arms he could not see distinctly. The creature continued to make a musical noise while he gazed about two minutes, and on perceiving him, it disappeared in an instant.

Chapter 3

MERMEN OF THE BRITISH ISLES

T he inhabitants of the British Isles have been a fishing and seafaring folk since earliest times. Not only did their ancient pantheon include a surfeit of water gods—including Lir and his son Manannan MacLir who wrapped himself in a cloak of sea mist—but tales of merfolk still abound up and down the countryside.

There may not be anyone today—from Land's End in Cornwall to the tip of John O' Groats in Scotland—who will claim to have actually seen a merman or water horse or sea trow. Yet stories about those mer creatures are still popular, and the literature of both Celtic and Anglo-Saxon heritages in the British Isles teems with such tales.

This account is from Master Walter Map's book *De Nugis Curialum* (A Courtier's Trifles). Map was an English priest and a witty storyteller at the court of Henry II, who collected folklore between 1181–1193. The text has been put into modern English by Frederick Tupper and Marbury Ogle Bladen.

Many yet alive report to us that they have seen in those waters a marvel, great beyond all wonder, Nicholas Pipe, a merman, who, without breathing, was wont to dwell on the floor of the ocean with the fishes. Detecting the approach of a storm, he forbade by his warning the sailing of ships from port or bade a return to those already under weigh. He was truly a man, with nothing monstrous in his limbs, and nothing lacking in his five senses, yet he received, in addition to human qualities, the endowment of fishes. But when he went down into the waters to make a stay there, he always carried with him pieces of old iron, wrenched away from a cart or from horses' hoofs or from old furniture—for what reasons I have not yet heard. In this one respect he was weaker than men and allied to fish, that he could not live without water or the smell of the sea. When he was led away some distance from it, he would run back as if with failing breath. William, King of Sicily, hearing of these things, wished to see him, and ordered him to be brought into his presence; but, when the men were dragging him along against his will, he died in their hands on account of absence from the sea. Although I have read and heard of things not less wonderful, I know of nothing exactly like this wonder.

The thirteenth-century writer Gervase of Tilbury swore that in his day, mermaids and mermen swarmed the seas surrounding Britain.

Another thirteenth-century scribe wrote, "fishes of strange shapes were taken, with helmets and shields like armed men, only they were much bigger," though he was more likely describing narwhales or swordfish or some kind of sharks.

According to the British historian Holinshed, a merman was captured in Orford in Suffolk, during the reign of King John. Captured in their nets by some sailors who were fishing, the merman was completely human in all his parts. For six months he was kept alive on a diet of raw fish and flesh, which he squeezed till all the moisture was removed. They tortured him and hung him up by his feet to get him to speak, but he never did. At last he "fledde sacretelye to the sea and neuer after seene nor heard off." Locally he is still remembered as "the Wild Man of Orford."

In the last year of the seventeenth century, a project was begun off the Isle of Man to search for drowned treasure using a diving bell. The man who descended in the bell returned overwhelmed with what he had seen: subterranean squares and streets lined with houses of crystal and mother-of-pearl, the floors studded with gems. He also spoke of "several comely mermen and beautiful mermaids who seemed frightened at my appearance and swam swiftly away."

Henry Reynolds, a Welsh farmer, recounted in 1782 seeing a being in the water that he first thought to be a youth of sixteen but on closer inspection had a tail, an unusually sharp nose, and "wild and fierce looks."

Near Buckie in Banffshire, in 1814, a schoolmaster wrote a letter about a merman that was printed in the *Aberdeen Chronicle*. He reported the creature as a merman "of a tawny colour appearing like a man sitting, with his body half bent... His countenance was swarthy, his hair short and curled, of a colour between a green and a grey." Further: "He had small eyes, a flat nose, his mouth was large, and his arms of an extraordinary length..."

In 1906, in Treland, several mermen were reported. The young man who saw the sea folk declared "they were shaped like a salmon from the waist down," but the older men with him described the merfolk as "just like Christians, only finer."

And as late as 1949, mermen were said to have been spotted off Craig More in Scotland by several crofters and sailors.

There are fishermen even today who will not utter certain words at sea, like the folk in Anstruther in the East Neuk of Fife in Scotland, who do not call a salmon by its name but rather "the pink fish," lest they displease the water gods. And other fishermen who still carry bits of food and silver to appease angry sea spirits. Or sailors who will not cross particular straits or pass a certain rock without whispering a protective charm.

Do they believe the tales? The mind says no. But the heart—that is a different matter altogether.

•••

In the Hebrides islands the existence of merfolk was once a

given. These mer were thought to possess magic belts or cinctures without which they could not swim under water. Any human coming upon such a belt and taking it up had the power to keep the mer creature land-bound.

In Scottish folklore, mermen were known by their red caps, which they wore while swimming among the breakers. The mermaids more regularly sunned themselves provocatively on rocks, wreaths of seaweed around their necks and shoulders. The mermen did most of the underwater work. If they became entangled in a fisherman's net and were not instantly released, they cast a death spell upon the neighborhood.

•••

One of the richest harvest of mermen stories comes from the Shetland Isles, the most northerly group of islands in Britain that sit high above the end of mainland Scotland, like a strand of pearls in the northern sea.

Shetlandic folklore is Scandinavian in character and feel, not to be wondered at given the history of the islands. In the sixth and seventh centuries their proximity to Norway was their peril, and they trembled time and again under the Viking swords.

"Oh Lord, protect us from the fury of the northmen," was a popular prayer, as the Vikings made off with women, children, cattle, goods.

But the Norsemen left behind something, too—a heritage of legend, story, myth. In some ways today's Shetlanders seem closer to their Norwegian forebears than their Scottish cousins. Certainly in their mer stories, the Norwegian fossegrim and nokken find counterparts.

Mar-Folk

The Shetlander—like so many people who live on intimate terms with the sea—once believed that beneath the waves lay an enchanted world of coral and crystal, eternal peace and joy. This Shetlandic underwater world was peopled with mar-folk.

The mar-folk spent their days swimming lazily through spacious halls and crystalline caves, in and out of aquatic forests and jeweled gardens.

Daily life among the mar-folk was quite mundane, not so different from the lives of the Shetlanders themselves. But when the mar-folk left their crystal palaces and traveled through the sea, they became half man, half fish.

The Icelandic mar-folk were reputedly small, well-proportioned, of a generous nature, and devoted to one another. Dark-complected with beards of various shades (brown, black, gray, red) the mar-men played exquisite melodies on flute and harp-like instruments. Unlike their mates, mar-men rarely came ashore.

The mar-folk's mischief was quite innocuous, which further distinguished them from other mermen: attaching a fisherman's hook to a rock or length of seaweed; taking the bait or the catch off a fisherman's hook.

However, sighting a mar-man was bad luck indeed, for it meant a storm at sea. (Though if the sailor was not noticed in turn by the mar-man, no evil actually resulted.)

The mar-man could also tell the future. If caught—a rare happenstance—the mar-man could be bargained with for a glimpse into what was in store.

Selchies

I am a man upon the land,
I am a selchie in the sea.

And when I'd far frae every strand,
My dwelling is in Sule Skerrie...

is a verse from the Scottish ballad "The Great Selchie of Sule Skerrie." (*Frae* means from; *strand*, beach; *skerrie*, sea rocks. *Selchie* is still a common Scottish term for seal.)

Child ballad number 113, it is one of the most familiar of the stories about the selchies, the seal folk, still popular around Scotland.

THE SEAL MAN
Orkney

A maiden dwelling in Norway married a seal-man named Hein Mailer. But right before the child was born, Mailer disappeared without a word of farewell. One day he was there, the next gone.

His wife took her infant son cradled in her arms and stood by the water. "Yer Daddy's to the sea," she cried. "Woe for ye and worse fer me."

Now her weeping and wailing did not stop, morning and night and one day a great seal rose up in the water not a yard from shore and addressed the weeping woman in human speech.

"I am a man on the land, wife. But now I am a seal in the sea. The sea is in my blood and it calls me home. Do not weep more."

She knew him at once, for he had Hein Mailer's eyes and Hein Mailer's voice. So she held the babe up and said, "Look on yer bairn, Hein Mailer. Do right by him, if not by me."

The seal nodded once and was gone.

For seven years she did not hear from him. And then one day he rose again a yard from shore and his wife said to her little laddie, "That is yer daddy, go give him a kiss."

This the boy did readily, never even minding the fishy smell, for he'd long been told who his father was and was well prepared to love him.

Hein Mailer placed a gold chain about the boy's neck, which allowed the lad to follow him on adventures in the sea, from which he always returned with wonderful tales to tell.

But one day, when he was just thirteen, the boy disappeared after his father and this time he did not return.

Eventually the woman remarried, a human who was not a fisherman but a fine gunner from far inland. She told him naught of her life before, for it was all like a dream. And indeed, sometimes she thought that was all it was.

One day in May he went out hunting and shot two seals—a young one and an old one. He skinned them and brought back the meat and fur to his wife.

"How strange, wife," he said, "for this gold chain was around the neck of the smaller seal. Here—it will look lovely on ye."

She screamed for she knew then what had seemed a dream was all too real. Putting a hand to her breast, she cried, "Alas, this weary fate that has been laid on me." And with one more shriek, she died, her heart broken in two.

One selchie legend holds that the seal—the gray seal in particular—was a human being returned to the sea. Another is that selchies were angels, fallen from grace but not wicked enough for hell, and so were sent to earth. But disenchanted with mankind, they chose the sea instead of land.

Most of the selchie stories agree that once the selchie doffed his or her coat of fur, he or she assumed a human form upon the land.

In Caithness in the Scottish Highlands, the exact origin of selchies is described in this story:

When the widowed King of Lochlinn married, his new wife, skilled in the Black Art, contrived to be rid of her stepchildren. After seven years and seven days, she effected a plan. She put them under a *geas*, a spell, transforming them into seals, neither flesh nor fish. At sea they would yearn for land, on land they would ache for the sea. Only three times a year, at full moon, would they be able to resume their human form.

In North Uist, an island in the Outer Hebrides in the northwest of Scotland, there is a clan known as the Macodrum of the Seal, because it was believed that members of this clan were descendants of a Macodrum who had married a selchie and had numerous progeny. These clan members are often distinguished by a thin membrane or webbing between their toes. Sometimes they have rough spots on the skin, throwbacks—it is said—to scales and fur.

In Ireland, on the coast of Donegal, there are several families who likewise consider themselves descendants of seals: O'Sullivan, Coneely, O'Flaherty, and Macnamara.

The Shetlanders believed selchies lived on or near a large rock or skerrie. During the seasonal changes, or when the moon waxed or waned, or during particular weather conditions, these selchies would swim to the shore, take off their skins, and dance. Being pack or group creatures who have a mystical bond with gulls, selchies often knew when hunters were approaching because a gull would circle overhead in warning. (Of course gulls being used as warning devices by a herd of basking seals—a well-documented behavior—probably gave rise to such stories.)

A singular aspect of all selchie tales is that it is the humans who are the victimizers, the selchies the victims.

One of the most famous Scottish selchie stories is this, from John O'Groat's, at the tip end of the country.

THE SEAL HUNTER AND THE SELCHIES
Scotland

Near John O'Groat's house, on the east coast of Scotland, lived a man who was a seal hunter who made his living selling skins. He never believed it was ill luck to do so. He laughed at such beliefs.

One day a stranger—massive and dark with a brooding face and gray eyes—arrived on horseback and waited near the seal hunter's house.

"Come out," he called. "My master wishes to do business with you."

Delighted at the prospect of a new customer, the seal hunter climbed onto the back of the horse, put his arms around the dark man's waist, and away they rode.

They galloped across the rocky ground and the seal hunter could scarcely catch his breath. The cold winter's wind blew before them. They overtook it. The cold winter's wind blew behind them. It could not catch them. They rode till they came to the sea's edge. Below was nothing but the sea stretched out before them like a leaden thing.

The stranger reined in his horse. "This is where my master dwells," he said, pointing down to the sea. Then he dismounted and, clasping the seal hunter in his arms, so tight the man could not move, the stranger leaped over the precipice into the sea.

Down and down and down they fell, past craggy rocks and into the cold waves; down and down and down through the gray water they fell, to the very bottom of the sea.

The seal hunter expected to drown. He hoarded the last bits of air in his lungs. Yet when that was gone, he found he was still alive, there under the sea.

How can this be? he wondered. But he did not dare ask.

Around and about them swam seals of every kind, young and old, male and female, gray and spotted and brown. The seal hunter realized at that same moment that his guide had turned into a seal, too.

When they reached the bottom, they came upon an old bull seal, moaning in pain. A thin trickle of blood skeined up through the water from a wound in his side.

"Here is my master," said the dark seal. Then he pointed to a bloody knife lying next to the wounded seal. "And that is your knife."

The seal hunter shuddered then, and remembered. Only hours before he had knifed a great bull seal that had escaped from him, plunging back into the sea, his knife still in its back.

"Your hand wounded him," said the stranger. "Only your hand can cure him."

Bitterly ashamed, the seal hunter bound up the great bull's wound with his own neckerchief. And in that instant, the old bull rose up again, hale and strong.

"I promise," the seal hunter said, surprised that the words came out of his mouth and not bubbles, "I will never hunt the seal again."

The guide took his hand and the two of them rose straight up to the water's surface. There the stranger once again took a man's shape, mounted his horse, helped the seal hunter up behind. Then they galloped back, faster than the wind, quieter than the earth, to the cottage where the stranger handed the seal hunter a bag of gold.

"Remember your promise," the stranger said. Then he was gone.

Keeping his word, the seal hunter never again killed a seal, and prospered ever after.

~

It is interesting to note that this same story is told by Gervase of Tilbury as happening in Provence to a group of sailors, one of whom wounds a porpoise. Suddenly a knight "born on a steed of the sea" gallops across the waters and demands the sailor to accompany him. He is brought below to heal a porpoise knight: "the guilty right hand gave aid to the wound." And of course from that time forth no sailors hunt porpoises.

An Aranmore sailor named Rogers in the nineteenth century was blown off course and landed in Scotland. He declared he'd met a man in a small cottage who showed him the scar of a wound he claimed Rogers had given him years before in a cove in Aranmore when he was a seal.

A tradition in the Faroe Islands talks of seals taking off their skins every ninth night and dancing on land in human form.

There is some scholarly debate about the origins of all these selchie stories. The most notable was forcibly argued by David MacRitche of Edinburgh, who pointed out that the early peoples of Finnish or sub-Arctic backgrounds often visited the northern isles in skin-boats or kayaks. Dressed in sealskin for the cold water passage, they took off their heavy outer clothing upon landing on the warmer islands. Typical boats can be found in the anthropological collections of some Scottish museums. Detractors, however, have pointed out that there are so many similar stories in places where the Finns did not visit, that this origin story is not wholly believable. Others further warn that it does not take into account the idea of totemic beliefs, i.e., the worship of seals as ancestral figures. Still it is a provocative theory and may be part of the puzzle.

Finns or Fin-Men
Somewhat like selchies, the finns of Shetland were more wizards than seals. They used their transformations as a

disguise. Like Eskimos, they dressed in sealskins and drove away the fish.

The male finns were daring boatmen who could chase fast sailing vessels far out into the ocean and all with a single sweep of the oars of their sealskin boats.

They were called finns or fin-men because they were thought to have originally come from Finland.

Sea Fairies

There are parts of Scotland where a belief in sea fairies is still strong. Sea fairies resembled seals. Covered with gray skin, they had lower limbs that were entirely a seal's, but above the waist were completely human. They reportedly lived in caves in the Land-Under-Waves. Lovers of music, they could be wooed to the surface when a piper played by the waterside, their sloe-eyes filling with delight. They had a language of their own (something rarely mentioned about other merfolk) yet were also well-versed in human speech. On shore they looked like humans with brown skin. At times they turned into horses, riding over mountain and moor.

From the Highlands also came the belief that merfolk—like the selchies—could put off their fishy coverings as the selchie puts off its coat of fur. Also, if a human found the scaly garment, and held it away, the owner was prevented from returning to the sea.

Blue Men

The Minch is a strait separating the Isle of Lewis from the mainland of Scotland and the Shiant Isles (the Charmed Islands). It is here alone that legends of the Blue Men appear, creatures the size of men but of superhuman strength. Like selchies, they swam in groups, deriving special delight in rising above the water to their waists.

The sound is also called "Drth nam Fear Gorm"—the Sound of the Blue Men—as well as "The Current of Destruction." Many people still sail around the Shiant Isles rather than take the short cut between them and the Isle of Lewis.

Scholars believe that the legends about the Blue Men arose from the incursions of Moroccan Berbers who sailed north to trade with the islanders, and whose faces were a glossy blue from the dye they used for their leather goods. When the trade in leather goods failed, many of the Berbers turned to piracy.

The Blue Men of the Minch—it was said—kept the waters of the Minch restless. Blue skinned, with long gray bearded faces, arms as restless as the waters, they rose up looking for sailing ships to plunder. Their attacks were called a "mad pleasure" by contemporary writers. But, fond of riddles, the Blue Men always allowed a ship safe passage if the captain were quick-witted enough to guess their word games. They were especially impressed with any human who could rhyme extemporaneously.

One tale tells of a ship coming upon a Blue Man fast asleep in the water. Taken aboard, he was bound hand and foot. But the ship had not sailed a thousand feet when two more Blue Men rose shouting:

Duncan will be one,
Duncan will be two,
Will you need another
Ere you reach the shore?

A moment later, as if he alone had understood the mysterious message, the prisoner snapped his bonds and leaped into the sea.

Finfolk

The Orcadians (from Orkney) not only peopled the sea with imaginary beings, but like their Shetland cousins imagined lush abodes beneath the waters. The Orcadian mermen lived in palaces that seem to come from descriptions from the Arabian *Thousand and One Nights*: sands of gold dust, walls of crystal and coral, adorned with pearls and precious stones, furniture of exquisitely wrought silver and gold, colors vying with the aurora borealis.

This magic land was Finfolkaheem—home of the finfolk. Human-looking beneath the waves, but fish-tailed, the finfolk could take the shape of any sea creature they chose.

Sea Trows

Sea trows are also from Orcadian and Shetlandic legend. "Great rolling creatures," they dwelled in vaulted sea-caverns. Often they alarmed fishermen by tumbling savagely close to the boats, thus forcing the sailors to use their oars to stave them off.

Scholars believe that the origin of sea trows may well have been porpoises.

The prince of the sea trows was called Allaritimus. Like a selchie, he could take off his gray skin and roam the land in human form.

King of the Auxcriniers

The Channel Island fishermen believed in a dwarf who lived below the water and knew the names and whereabouts of all who had been drowned. He was described by Victor Hugo this way in the novel *The Toilers of the Sea*:

> His head is massive in the lower part and narrow in the forehead; his squat and corpulent figure; his skull, covered with warty

excrescences; long legs, long arms, fins for feet, claws for hands, and a sea-green countenance... He has a stiff spreading beard, running with water, and overlapping a sort of pelerine, ornamented with fourteen shells, seven before and seven behind.

The King of the Auxcriniers foretold every major storm, and rising above the waves, his face lit up with an evil smile.

Shellycoat

A violent water demon who is a gigantic monster, Shellycoat was so named because he wore a coat of shells which rattled horribly when he flew through the air. But after any great adventure, Shellycoat left his garment under a rock, which rendered him helpless.

He was said to haunt the banks of the Ettrick River, crying out as if he were drowning, then jeering at anyone who came to his rescue.

Fintan

Fintan was the first Irish merman. He came to Ireland before the flood and was saved in the form of a fish though he lived on shore in human form.

Eventually Fintan was converted to Christianity by St. Patrick. Not surprisingly, Fintan became a saint himself.

Old sculptures show him looking a great deal like paintings of the Babylonian water god, Ea-Enki.

Anfacs

These are Welsh water spirits who produced both excessive wet weather and floods.

One tale is told of Llyn y Fan Fach, where a huge hairy fellow with a hideous face emerged from a watercourse when people began digging nearby. He stormed at them and cried that if they did not leave him alone, he would drown the entire town. A similar story in Llyn Cwm Llwch has the anfac dressed in red and sitting on a chair upon the waters of the lake.

Water Kelpie
Also known as the water horse, this Scottish and Welsh spirit could appear as a horse or a handsome young man.

In horse form, the kelpie haunted fords and pools and tried to carry away unwary travelers. Waiting till someone mounted his back, he then rode off with them into the water where they drowned. But if a bridle on which the sign of a cross had been carved was thrown over the water horse's head, he could be made to carry stones to build a mill or steading. It was said that such a bridled kelpie helped build the church of St. Vigeans, about a mile outside the town of Arbroath.

There's an old rhyme that supposedly was spoken by a kelpie working in such a bridle:

> Sair back and sair banes,
> Carrying the Laird of Morphy's stanes.

Kelpies also could make the waters of a lake or waterfall flood and in that way overwhelm travelers.

It was possible to kill a kelpie, but difficult. A blacksmith and his family terrorized by such a creature heated two iron spits and drove them into the kelpie's flanks. That did the trick, iron being anathema to fairy creatures.

THE SERVANT GIRL AND THE KELPIE
Wales

Once long ago a servant girl went with her master's cattle to the side of the loch. While they grazed, she sat down on the bank to eat her meal of bread and cheese.

After a while, she saw a handsome young man come along the waterside, and he stopped before her and asked in a soft, persuasive voice, "Would you comb my hair, young miss?"

She nodded shyly, and he lay down by her and put his head in her lap, on the apron. She took out her comb and began to comb out his thick, black locks when—to her horror—she found a certain weed that abounds only in ponds.

She knew then that he was none other than a kelpie, a water horse, and if she did not keep her wits about her, he would surely drown her.

"Close your eyes a bit," she said to him, "and I will make your hair as soft and ruly as my master's own."

So he closed his eyes and was soon fast asleep.

As soon as she could see he was sleeping, the servant girl untied her apron strings and slipped out of it, leaving the water spirit still asleep. Then she ran home as fast as ever she could. When she was near the house, she gave a glance behind and saw him coming after her in the likeness of a horse. But she gained the house and shut the door behind. As there was a cross over the lintel, he could not come in and he eventually went away.

～

Shoopiltee
This is the Shetland kelpie who in horse form entices riders and then gallops off into the sea.

Dooinney Marrey
The merman of the Isle of Man could be kept from a boat as long as it carried "coul iron" or cold iron, in the shape of nail in the mast or some such. He could occasionally be helpful too, and give the fishermen warning of an oncoming storm, as long as they appeased him with a tot of rum over the side of the boat.

Uruisg

A large Scottish waterman who frequently haunted waterfalls and even—some said—lived under them. Like the helpful brownies, he gave aid to farmers by threshing and grinding corn. But sometimes he was more dangerous, especially because he was extremely stupid and always falling in love with human women.

In human form, he often wooed unwed maidens. But a lass who knew what to look for—waterweed or rush in his hair, for example—might escape his deadly embrace.

Tangie

A sea sprite from Orkney, he was named for the tang or seaweed with which he was covered. Sometimes he appeared as a man, other times as a horse.

Merrows

Merrows (or *murrughach, moruadh,* or *moruach* in Gaelic) were the Irish counterparts of mermaids and mermen. As with other merfolk, the merrow males were extremely ugly, with green teeth and hair, sharp red noses, piggy eyes, and finny arms.

When on shore, the merrow wore red caps so they were hard to miss, even if you did not notice their green teeth or hair or sharp red noses. The red caps held the charm that allowed them to pass from their dry underwater world, through the water to land.

On the other hand, merrow women were beautiful enchantresses, except for—as William Butler Yeats points out in *Irish Fairy and Folk Tales*—their fish tails and the scale between their fingers.

The merrows lived in an encapsulated dry world under the sea and to see one foretold a gale. They kept drowned sailors in "soul-cages," which resemble lobster pots. In the Irish story "The Soul Cages," the merrow says,

> I've only when I see a good storm coming on, to set a couple dozen of these, and then, when the sailors are drowned and the souls get out of them under the water, the poor things are almost perished to death, not being used to the cold; so they make into my pots for shelter, and then I have them snug and I fetch them home, and keep them here dry and warm...

Roane
These are the Highland mermen who swim through the water as seals. Like selchies, they can shed their skins, and cannot go back into the water without them.

These creatures are mild-mannered, and in Katharine Brigg's words, "of deep domestic affections."

Fuaths
High in the Scottish mountain streams lived the yellow-haired fuaths, malevolent underwater folk who delighted in drowning mortals. Like their fairy cousins, the web-footed fuaths wore green and feared cold iron.

A fuath could be identified by his shock of yellow hair, the webbing between his toes, his tail, and the fact that he had no nose. It was not easy to mistake him.

Davy Jones
According to Tobias Smollet in his novel *The Adventures of Peregrinbe Pickle*, he is "a fiend that presides over all the evil spirits of the deep and is seen in various shapes, warning the devoted wretch of death and woe." It is in his "locker" or cupboard that the spirits of drowned sailors are kept.

Some scholars think his name is a corruption of the Indian Deva, a water god. Others that—like the British rivers Tavy and Taff—it derives from the Celtic root word *tau* or *taff,* which means watercourse. (*See* page 91.)

Water Leaper

A Welsh water spirit, the water leaper—or as it is known in Welsh "ILamhigyn y Dwr"—was a pesty spirit who bothered fishermen even into the nineteenth century. He took the flies off fisherman's hooks, scared away the fish, and sometimes even pulled on the line with such force, the fisherman himself was dragged into the deep water.

The water leaper resembled a toad, except that it had wings and a tail and could shriek with such force, it could split a fisherman's bone to the marrow.

Spirits of the Wells

Throughout Britain, wells have been thought to be the repository of water spirits who were also well known healers. There have been volumes written about them. As Janet and Colin Bord write in *Sacred Waters*: "...there is strong evidence of gods associated with water and with the underworld in the form of ritual pits, shafts, or wells, of which over a hundred have been excavated in Britain."

Often there were customs of sacrifice associated with the water spirits; throwing gifts or offerings into the wells was a custom that ran from Neolithic times right up to our present day when people still throw coins into wishing wells. Many of these spirits seem to be mother goddesses. But a number were male.

For example, on the river Trent, the tidal wave is known locally as "Eager," most likely a corruption of the Scandinavian god Aegir. When the river was in flood, the local Nottingham bargees used to call out, "Look out, Eager is coming!"

MERMEN OF SOUTHERN EUROPE

In the southern waters, stories of mermen are scarce, except in Greece where the sea gods like Oceanus and Poseidon and his followers have held the imaginations for centuries.

In Pliny's *Natural History*, however, was this account testified to by knights of Rome:

> ...in the coast of the Spanish Ocean neer unto Gades, they have seen a Mere-man, in every respect resembling a man as perfectly in all parts of the bodie as might be. And they report, moreover, that in the night season he would come out of the sea abord their ships; but look upon what part soever he setled, he waied the same downe, and if he rested and continued there any long time, he would sinke it cleane.

Oceanus

According to Greek tradition, all the water elements came from Oceanus. His sister consort was Tethys and they had 3,000 aquatic daughters.

Poseidon and the Tritons

Poseidon was the Greek god of the sea. Fish-tailed breeder of horses and bulls, inventor of ships, he was god of all the waters: oceans, sea, rivers, streams, pools, springs, wells. Huge, majestic, and muscular, he was Zeus's brother and his equal in power. It was said that he created the first horse by striking a rock with his trident. Usually represented as a bearded man with a fish tail, he rode the foam in a shell chariot drawn by frisking dolphins.

In love with Amphitrite, he wooed her by using the dolphin Delphinius as a messenger. Three children came from that union: his son Triton and two daughters. He also sired a group of monsters, including the winged horse Pegasus, and was father of the hero Theseus as well.

Son Triton was a man to the waist with a dolphin's tail. It was his job to raise storms and calm the seas. He lived with his parents in a golden palace under the sea near Aegae in Euboia, though the mythical lake Tritonis near the Mediterranean coast of Libya was said to be his favorite residence.

Triton raised the goddess Athena as a companion to his own daughter Pallas.

Leader of a group of fish-tailed mermen, who all formed part of Poseidon's retinue, Triton lent his name to the group who are collectively known as tritons.

Scaly bodied, the tritons had sharp teeth and hands ending in fierce claws. Usually pictured rushing about, long hair streaming behind, a choppy sea in their wake, they were most often associated with the malevolent aspects of the sea.

Some tritons—*centaurotritons* or *icthyotauri*—were pictured in mosaics and painted on pottery with the forefeet of horses and with a fish tail.

All tritons were said to play loudly upon conch shells as Poseidon approached. But unlike mermen of other lands, the tritons had no other musical ability.

Scholars muse that the tritons may have originated because of a confusion between the old fish gods of western Asia—Dagon and Oannes—but in the end became merely bogies in tales to frighten children.

In the second century, the Greek travel writer Pausanias swore he had seen a triton in Rome, with hair on its head like a marsh frog, sharkskin scales on its body, fang-like teeth, a dolphin's tail, and long-fingered hands with sharp nails. To top it off, Pausanias declared the beast had bright blue eyes.

And in Pliny's *Natural History*, was this report of a triton:

In the time that Tiberius was Emperour, there came unto him an ambassador from Ulissipon, sent of purpose to make relation, That upon their sea-coast there was discovered within a certain hole, a certain sea goblin, called Triton, sounding a shell like a trumpet or cornet, and that he was in forme and shape like those that are commonly painted for Tritons.

Proteus

Old Man of the Sea, Proteus was a smelly old shapeshifter who slept with the seals. If caught, he would change shapes in quick succession, but if a person held on, Proteus would reveal the future. There are many stories in which a shapeshifter caught changes form rapidly—as in the Scottish "Tam Lin"—but the Greek Proteus is thought to be the prototype of them all.

Drakos

These Greek well spirits—often giants—can be found throughout Greek mythology. While inclined to eat people, they are quite stupid and can often be tricked.

Other well spirits, however, are much deadlier. In Chios, for example, the well spirits are sometimes known as "Arabs." They are demons (called "master of the well") who pull down anyone who leans too far over the edge. In Macedonia, a popular folk ballad called "The Haunted Well" ends with "Do not tell my mother I am dead / Tell her, brothers, that I am married / Black Earth is my wife, a tombstone is my mother-in-law / The fine grass blades my brothers and sisters-in-law." Those last two lines are staples in Greek folklore.

THE HAUNTED WELL
Macedonia

There were nine brothers who went off in the service of their king to fight the Franks.

"Your blessing, dear mother," the nine asked before they left.

"Milk and honey in your path," said their old mother.

"May nine go out but eight come back. Let John the youngest marry well and not return." Then she hugged them all, but for her favorite, young John, she reserved her kisses.

Off they went, as if on a jolly lark, riding on their horses across a vast plain. Young John's horse was called the Black One.

They lived forty days without bread and forty-five without water, until they came upon a well thirty fathoms deep in the middle of the plain.

Eight of the brothers wanted to drink, but John cried out for them to stop.

"There is a spirit living in the well," he cried. "Who knows if it means us ill."

The brothers stopped, and one said, "Then we must choose lots to see who will go down."

They broke off nine sticks, eight long and one short, then each drew a stick from the oldest brother's hand. The short one fell to young John.

So they lowered him down into the well on a rope and when they went to draw him up again, the rope was heavier than before.

"A serpent has wound himself round my body," John cried. "He is an evil spirit. Tie the rope to the Black One's saddle and draw me out."

So they tied the rope around the pommel of the saddle and John's loyal horse strained to pull him out. Slowly the rope rose and at last John rose, too, wrapped in the serpent's awful coils. But try as his brothers might, they could not kill the serpent with their knives, for he was a spirit and not of this world.

"Give me a knife, brothers," cried John. "Give me a sword."

They threw him a sword and he said to them, "Leave me my brothers and go home. Tell our mother I am married to Black Earth for a wife, that a tombstone is my mother-in-law, and the fine grass blades are my wife's brothers and sisters." Then he drew the sword across the rope, cutting it in two and fell back down into the well.

~

Neptune

The Roman version of Poseidon was Neptune, but he was a relatively late arrival. First mentioned only in 399 BC when a festival was ordained for him, it was over two hundred years more before he had a temple built in his honor. His attributes are directly connected to the older Greek god, Poseidon.

Neptune was usually pictured rising up from the waves that foamed around his great fish tail. He carried a trident with which he could shatter rocks or call up storms. It was said that he bred the first horse.

Beiseiglia Merman

The other famous Italian merman was a fishboy born in Beiseiglia, Italy, in 1684. His parents, Peter Anthony Consiglio and Elizabeth Nastasia, gave this account of his birth.

When born, the boy was quite covered with the scales of a fish, having nevertheless a beautiful and comely neck and face with no unseemly colour. His head was adorned with curious flaxen hair and from the neck down to the sole of his foot, his is all over blackish and hairy intermixt with spots of several sorts and colours like the scales of a fish.

He is of human stature and tender-limbed. The bottoms of his feet are white and so are the insides of his hands, like unto shells of a sea tortoise. He is about ten year of age and is named Barnardin.

Elizabeth kept her son's condition secret for many years, saying prayers over him and washing him frequently, but to no avail. His hairy skin did not change. But because of it, he was taken away to Holland and educated above his station. By the time he was an adolescent, he spoke Italian, French, and Low Dutch. His condition was sworn to by Dutch physicians. Catering to humanity's morbid curiosity, his keepers put him on show where he was seen by royalty as well as by the common folk. In London he was exhibited at the house of Mr. Barton, a milliner near the "His Royal Highness Coffee House" in Charing Cross.

Poor Barnardin was probably not a merman at all but a child with an unfortunate number of birth defects, still his story has come down to us as the "Merman of Beiseiglia," the only one of his kind in the southern seas.

Drac

The French version of the dracae lived in caverns under the rivers. Often they floated on the water's surface disguised as gold rings or cups or richly carved wooden dishes. They were interested not only in women, but in young boys who bathed in the water. Most often taken by the drac, however, were women still suckling their children. They were brought below the water to act as wet nurse to the drac's wife's babies. After three or seven years, the captured women would be released to return to their old homes, where they were sometimes not remembered or recognized by those they had left behind.

According to Gervaise of Tilsbury, one such nursemaid happened to put her fingers into an eel pasty the drac had given her to eat, and then by mistake placed her hand on her eye. Suddenly she

> became endowed with most clear and distinct vision under the water. When her three years was up, and she had returned to her family, she met the Drac in the marketplace of Beaucaire. She knew him at once, and saluting him, inquired about the health of her mistress and the child. To this the Drac replied, "Hark ye, with which eye do you see me?" She pointed to the eye she had touched with the fat: the Drac immediately thrust his finger into it and he was no longer visible to any one.

Of course this is a much repeated story in Great Britain, with its own tale type number, only instead of a drac, the creature is usually a fairy.

Drowned Men

In Brittany's Baie des Trepasses, it is said that all the men who drowned that year held a yearly gathering. They rose up on the white crests of the waves, looking for drowned friends. When two such souls finally met, they whispered back and forth, which is what anyone nearby heard as a soft susurration of the sea.

This account of a Portuguese fisherman was also in the French *Journal Encylopedique*, "Observations on Mermen":

> Off the Comoryn Coast, Portuguese fishermen netted a merman. They promptly brought him to King Emmanuel. He refused to eat and was on the verge of dying when the king decided to attach a light chain to him and allow him to cavort in the water. He was transported with joy. So he lived for several years. The observers found him intelligent and graceful but in all that time it was not possible to teach him a single word.

Chapter 5

MERMEN OF ASIA

In China, Japan, and India, and the smaller nations around them, there are considerable numbers of stories that take place in kingdoms under the sea. Most often the gods who rule there are dragons (or in India, the Naga monarch, a quasi-dragon) and they are almost always spoken of as masculine.

Except for the Dragon mother who gave birth to them all, the rulers in these stories are all male. Often, however, the dragon kings have beautiful daughters who are not dragons—and the tales that revolve around these maidens usually involve a human suitor.

In both Japan and China, this land under the water could be entered either through deep mountain caves or through a dragon-guarded well. Often the palace was said to be under a particularly remote island in the Eastern Sea and protected by towering crags, though sometimes there was a red light burning above the island as a signal.

As Japan is an island nation, it has many different kinds of water spirits, some benevolent, some malevolent. The stories that are told about these watermen differ from island to island. There are still many shrines in use in Japan that are dedicated to one water deity or another.

Sagara

The Japanese dragon king Sagara lived in the ocean and owned a white pearl known as "Pearl of the Ebb Tide" and a blue pearl known as "Pearl of the Flood Tide" as well as a pearl that granted all desires.

In one story about Sagara, the Empress Jingo sent her ships to obtain tribute from Korea. A huge Korean fleet set sail to counter that threat. Sagara cast down the "Pearl of the Ebb Tide" and the waters immediately disappeared, leaving both sides stranded. Whereupon the King of Korea and all his men leaped onto the flat seabed and started running toward the Japanese fleet. At that very moment, Sagara flung the "Pearl of the Flood Tide" onto the ocean bottom and the waters came flooding back. Later Sagara presented the Tide Pearls on a pink seashell to Empress Jingo's son Prince Onjin.

Sagara had many other names: Oho-wata-tsumi, "Sea Lord," and Toyo-tama hiko no Mikoto, or "Abundant Prince of Pearls," are two of them. He was once so feared, that sailors threw jewels over the side of their ships to appease him.

Kompira

Another famous Japanese water god, Kompira was an ugly, big-bellied god who sat cross-legged under the waves. Once a demon, he had been won over to Buddhism and ever after became the god of happiness. Sailors adopted him as their own special deity and at one time almost all Japanese ships carried a charm from his shrine.

Kappas

Long-haired Japanese water monsters, the kappas had tortoise bodies, scaly limbs, and monkey-like faces. They liked to cover mares and drown humans. Catching an unwary traveler, the kappa dragged him underwater and sucked out his blood. The kappa's favorite mode of transportation was said to be a flying cucumber.

Occasionally a kappa was befriended by a wise man to whom he taught the setting of bones. Another popular story in Japan is about a friendly kappa who borrows a family's rice bowl and returns it intact, after which they are rewarded with riches.

Pond-Snail

In Japan there are numerous variants of a story in which a pond demigod in the shape of a snail marries a village girl and turns into a handsome young man.

In fact, in some areas of the country, villagers used to believe that pond snails were either the deity or his messengers and prayed to them for protection against fire and for rain.

THE POND SPIRIT
Japan

In the garden of an old palace that once belonged to the Emperor Yozei was a pond. This story takes place long after the emperor was dead and the palace grounds were filled with new houses. Only the pond remained. But it had been a long time since the pond had been dredged and it was grown over with weeds and quite noxious.

One night, a man who drank too much sake could not find his way home, and he lay down on a veranda by the pond to sleep. It was a warm summer night, so he was in no danger of freezing to death. But as he lay there, some creature bent over him and felt his face.

That touch so frightened the would-be sleeper, he kept quiet and pretended to snore. But as soon as the creature walked away from him, the sleeper opened his eyes. He saw a small man, not three feet tall, who walked over to the pond's edge, dove in, and did not come back up again.

Well, this was too much for the man, who sobered up at once. He ran away from the veranda and into the street where he told the first people he met what had just happened.

"That same thing has occurred every night this week," said one fellow. "No one wants to sleep by the pond any more."

"My father-in-law owns that property," said another. "If we could get rid of that little nuisance, he would pay a goodly sum."

But none of them would volunteer, for they were all shivering with fear.

"It must be some sort of kappa," they agreed. "A monster who will eat you alive."

But the sake drinker thought to himself, "I could use a reward. I don't believe in kappas anyway and if this one had really wanted to eat me, I would already be dead." So he nodded his head and said out loud, "Give me a piece of rope and I'll catch him."

So they found him a rope and he went back to the pond side and lay down once again while the other men all hid behind a wall to watch.

This time the sake drinker had a long wait, till well past midnight. He had actually started to doze off when the little man was suddenly there by his side, feeling his face.

The sake drinker leaped up, grabbed the rope, and twisted it three times around the little man, then tied the rope end to a nearby railing.

"I've got him," he cried out. "Bring a light!"

Shaking with fear, the other men brought out a light. And when they held it up, they could see the creature really wasn't a monster at all, but a man only three feet high, dressed in pale yellow who blinked at them as if the light hurt his eyes.

"Please," said the little man, "you have me tied tight, but I am so thirsty. It must be the fear. Could you bring me a tub of water?"

The man whose father-in-law owned the property said, "What harm could it do? We still have him bound."

So they brought out a tub of water and the little man

leaned over as much as he could, given that he was still tied to the railing. It seemed as if he were looking at his reflection in the water.

The men started to laugh, but the little man spoke again.

"I'm a water spirit," he said to them, as if that explained everything. Then he collapsed into the tub.

The knotted rope floated on the top of the water, and the tub was suddenly overflowing, but of the little man there was no sign at all.

The sake drinker realized that the little man had only wanted fresh water in his pond, nothing more. So he dumped the tub into the pond, cleaned out the weeds, and the little man was never seen again.

≈

Awabi

These sea demons lived near Nanao, Japan, and ate drowned fishermen. It was they who guarded the great seashells that contained shining jewels.

Drifted Deities

In Japan a group of water spirits known as drifted deities are said to have drifted ashore in the long ago from a region far over the sea. These deities may have been brought to shore by the waves, by fishermen who found them in their nets, in canoes or boats made of peachtree wood, on the back of an octopus or shark or tortoise, in seaweed, or in the stomach of a whale. There is even a story in which a drifted deity came ashore in a sake barrel.

A stone was considered the object in which the deity lived, and the stone usually became the center of an altar or shrine. Such a stone was called *kami-kata-ishi* or "symbolic stone of the deity."

Ebisu Saburo

Ebisu is a god believed to be the protector of different occupational groups, one of the Seven Deities of Good Luck. Sometimes depicted as a fisherman with a red snapper under his arm, sometimes a shark or whale or a fishing float tied to a net, or even a corpse floating in the water, Ebisu Saburo is a spirit of good fortune and wealth for fishermen. He is considered one of the "drifted deities" sacred to the fishing communities. Fishermen in certain districts of Japan have Ebisu altars in their homes.

There are also a number of sacred stones said to be images of Ebisu.

Samebito

Half man, half shark, Samebito (*same* means "shark") was a black monster with glowing green eyes and a spiky beard. There is a story that when he was expelled from the ocean, he was rescued by the Japanese hero Totaro who brought the monster to a lake near his castle. Years later, when Totaro lay dying of grief because the girl he wished to marry had an impossibly high bride price of 10,000 precious jewels, Samebito shed tears that were rubies, emeralds, and pearls. This enabled his benefactor to marry the girl he loved.

Dragons

The Chinese dragons had "the head of a camel, the horns of a stag, the eyes of a demon, the ears of a cow, the neck of a snake, the belly of a clam, the scales of a carp, the claws of an eagle, the soles of a tiger," or so ancient writers claimed.

Chinese dragons were shape-changers. As humans, they were fat old men with long beards, heavy moustaches, and enormous eyebrows. They could also turn into an animal: rat, snake, fish.

Or an implement: weapon, shovel. But they were always associated with water, whether rain, ponds, rivers, oceans.

Supposedly Chinese dragons slept in their pools in the winter, rising to fight in the spring. This battle brought about thunderstorms and cleansing, healing rains. Of course if too many dragons were in the battle, the rains turned to flood and instead of helping the land, the land was ravaged by the waters.

Besides the great dragons, there were lesser gods of rivers, such as Hopo, known as Count of the River, who demanded the sacrifice of young maidens of noble blood.

GREEN DRAGON POND
China

A dragon lived in an ice-cold pond below the Malong peak in Dali. He was the kind of dragon who could change himself into a man and only did good deeds. And because he was so benevolent, the people near the pond lived long, peaceful, contented lives.

Now on one side of the pond there was a temple in which a monk and his two novices lived. The monk was very religious, and he could recite long passages of the scriptures. But he was also a passionate chess player, and it was because of this that an awful fate befell the temple.

During a spring rain, a handsome, well-dressed young man came to the temple gate and asked for shelter from the shower. This the monk granted, and when he found out the young man played chess, the monk was delighted.

"I am not a good player," the young man warned.

"To be falsely humble," said the monk, "is the worse kind of pride."

The young man smiled. If the monk noticed such things, he

would have seen that the smile had too many teeth.

They sat down to play, and it was soon apparent the young man had—indeed—been too humble. For the first time in many years, the old monk had met his match. But the rain stopped before the game was over, and the young man stood up.

"I must go back home, Master," he said.

"Oh do not…" the monk began.

"If I may, I shall return tomorrow and learn what I can from you."

•••

Early the next day, the young man returned and he played many games with the old monk. Some the monk won, some he lost. He and the young man were evenly matched. And so a friendship was struck up between the two.

Half a year went by before the monk began to puzzle about his friend who always seemed to have so much time on his hands. One day he asked, "What is it you do, my young friend that you have so much time for me? Do you not have work? Do you not have a family?"

The young man gave a toothy smile, and said, "Since we are friends, there must be truth between us. I live quite close to your temple. The Green Pond is my home."

"But no man can live in a pond," protested the monk.

"Quite correct," said the young man. "I am not really a man at all. I am a dragon. A dragon who was lonely for a friend."

This the old monk could not believe, and he said so.

"Come with me to the pond and I will prove it to you," said the young man.

He took the monk by the hand and led him to the pond. There, fully clothed, he dived into the water and did not come back up.

The monk gazed into the cold, deep water and trembled. What should he do? How could he rescue the young man who—he suddenly realized—must be quite mad. He was about to run back to the temple and call for his novices and a rope, when the young man suddenly surfaced, a silver plate in his hand. He got out of the water, shook himself once, and stepped ashore.

The old monk noticed with awe that he had not a drop of water on him. His clothes, his shoes—even his hair—were dry.

"Master, for the many days of pleasure your company has brought me, please accept this gift," the young man said, holding out the platter. On it lay a magnificent robe.

Trembling, the old monk refused. "I am not worthy of such a gift."

The young man laughed, and this time the monk could see how many teeth he had. "Who was it who told me at our first meeting that to be falsely humble is the worst kind of pride? Take the robe. Some day you will find it useful."

The old monk took the robe, but he did not put it on.

•••

From then on, the friendship between the two deepened and every day—with the exception of times when the Green Dragon had to make rain—they played chess and talked about the world and the creatures on it.

One fateful morning, in the middle of a chess game, the old monk said, "I believe you when you tell me you are a dragon, but why then do you look just like a man?"

"Because an ordinary man is not allowed to look upon a dragon. You would be terrified and would die from the sight."

"But we are as close as brothers, Green Dragon," said the old monk. "Of course outsiders should not see you in all your glory. But am I not different?" He put down his chess piece with care.

Still the dragon refused.

•••

After this, at every game, every day he saw Green Dragon, the old monk made the same request, till at last Green Dragon said, "It is not just that you would be terrified, Master. But once a man sees me, I will never be able to become human again. All the good deeds I have done for so many years will disappear as well."

The old monk scratched his head. "But surely the proscription does not include a Buddhist monk."

Green Dragon smiled sadly. "A monk is still a man. However our friendship must count for something. And if you put on the magical robe I gave you..." He hesitated. "Wait! There are others here at the temple, and they could be in danger."

This time it was the old man's turn to smile. "Leave that to me. I will send my novices off to town to get supplies. We can lock the gate. I only need to see you in your dragon shape once. Please..." And though he didn't realize it, the old man suddenly sounded like a young child wheedling for extra sweets.

The young visitor nodded, but there was no joy in his eyes.

•••

Early next morning, the old monk sent his novices into town with a long list of supplies. "Do not hurry back," he called after them.

And as soon as the boys were out of sight, Green Dragon arrived at the gate.

The old monk hurried out to greet him wearing the magical robe. "Now, Green Dragon, quick. Show me your dragon form."

Green Dragon said some words under his breath and, without a breath more, the young man was gone and on the ground lay a long, skinny, green snakelike creature with two tiny horns on its head.

"Is this it?" asked the monk, when he could speak again. "This tiny thing is the famous Green Dragon?" His voice was full of disappointment.

The snake suddenly disappeared and the familiar young man stood before him. "Master, I did not wish to frighten you. I can be as large or as small as I like."

"You will not frighten me, my boy," said the monk, suddenly puffed up with something akin to pride. "Do your worst. Let me see you in all your enormity."

The old monk's words flattered the Green Dragon and he said quietly, "I will."

•••

Now as the young man prepared to turn himself into the great dragon, down the road the two novices had suddenly decided to go back for they were worried about their master.

"Master seemed so strange today," said one.

"He certainly seemed in a hurry to get rid of us," said the other.

"And he was certainly in no hurry to have us return," said the first.

They started at a slow trot that soon became a run and

reached the gate just as the Green Dragon was beginning to change. But the gate was locked and, push as they might, they could not open it. So standing on tiptoes, they peeked through some holes in the wood.

•••

The word being spoken, the Green Dragon began his change. First he turned into the small green snake. Then, hissing a new word, he began to grow and grow and grow some more till he was as large as a cart, then as large as a house, then as large as a ship on the sea.

The two novices were at first enthralled, then a bit frightened. They backed away from the gate and looked up just as the dragon's head cleared the top of gate and stared down at them.

They screamed, and the dragon screamed back, killing them both with the sound.

At the same time, the heavens opened up and rain flooded down, raining so hard, the Green Dragon Pool overflowed its banks and broke down the temple gates. It carried the old monk away and destroyed the temple.

If it had not been for his magic robe, the old man would have drowned. But he was so chastened by what had happened, he never went back to the area again, but wandered with a begging bowl for the rest of his life to atone for his great sin of pride.

As for the Green Dragon, he regretted his carelessness so bitterly, he wept until he was carried away by the same flood into Dali lake where he lived forever in dragon form.

And if you do not believe me, go to the Malong peak. There you will see the pond and near it a square of stone where the temple once stood. Anyone you meet will tell you this same sad tale.

～

Nagas
Like the Chinese dragons, the Indian nagas in Hindu mythology are semi-divine beings with human heads and serpent bodies who live under the water in a city called Bhagavati. There they are surrounded by dancing girls and flowers.

The nagas only harm humans if the humans mistreat them. They possess both deadly venom and the elixir of life.

Karkotaka, king of the nagas, can control the weather.

Deva
In India, not only the nagas are associated with water. Some scholars believe that Deva, a water god, is the progenitor somehow of the English "Davy Jones' locker," which is the place underwater where drowned sailors go. (*See* page 65.)

THE FISH PRINCE
India

Once there was a Rajah and a Ranee who longed for a child but could not have one. Because she was childless, the Ranee became more and more melancholy till at last she could take pleasure in nothing.

Now one day some fish were brought to the palace kitchen for a great dinner the Rajah was giving. Among them was the oddest fish the cook had ever seen. It had rainbow colored scales—red and green and yellow and blue—that were not dimmed by its being out of water. There was also a mark upon its head that looked, so the cook thought, like a little golden crown.

Oddest of all, the fish could talk. "Do not kill me," it said, "but put me in a basin of water and carry me to the Ranee, for I will surely amuse her."

The cook brought the fish at once to the Ranee's door and her maid brought it to the Ranee herself. And the Ranee was, indeed, amused by the little talking fish. She kept it close, both day and night, and soon she became so fond of it, she could not have loved it more had it been her own child, so she named it Muchie Rajah, or the Fish Prince.

Before long, the Fish Prince was too large for the basin, so the Ranee had him put in a marble bath. And when he was too big for that, she had a great tank made for him in the garden.

Every day she would take some rice out to visit the Fish Prince and he would put his head up out of the water and eat the rice from her hand.

A year went by and then another, and then one day when the Ranee went into the garden to talk to the Fish Prince, he did not rise up when she called. He simply lay at the bottom of the tank, looking dull and lifeless.

"Aiyee, my son," the Ranee cried, "what is wrong? Are you sick?"

He rose slowly to the surface and gasped out, "Not sick, mother, but dying of loneliness for a maiden of my own age. I beg you to build a little room by the side of my tank and bring a young girl to live in it. She will be company for me when you are busy."

So the Ranee did what he asked, and sent for stonemasons to build a charming little house that was so cleverly designed, the Fish Prince could put his head up over the wall and yet no water would ever overflow into the room itself. The walls of the house were covered with beautiful carvings and precious stones, and there were hanging lamps made of onyx and pearl.

Only when she was satisfied with the house did the Ranee send messengers throughout the kingdom to find the perfect girl to marry the Fish Prince. To the parents of such a prize, the Ranee declared she would give a lac of gold mohurs.

But alas—no parents in the kingdom were willing, even for so much gold, to part with a daughter to be a bride to a fish, for they all suspected that the Fish Prince—who had grown to an enormous size—only wished to devour the girl, not marry her.

Now not far from the palace lived a sadhu whose wife had died in childbirth, leaving him to raise their daughter Balna alone. When Balna was thirteen, the sadhu married again, but to a woman whose own daughter was as ugly and mean-tempered as Balna was beautiful and kind.

Of course the stepmother hated Balna and would have done anything to get rid of her.

So when the sadhu was off on a journey, the stepmother sent for the Ranee's messengers, saying, "I have just the girl for you. I am certain that your Fish Prince will find her delectable. And do not forget the gold mohurs." Then she went into the back of the house and told Balna that she was to be the bride of the Fish Prince in the morning.

Balna began to weep, "My father would never have sold me thus," she cried, but the stepmother was adamant.

"Go to the river and wash your best sari. Tomorrow you are to be a bride."

There was nothing Balna could do, for in those days daughters always obeyed their parents. She went down to the river and began to wash her sari, but she wept as she did it, great heaving sobs.

A seven-headed cobra lived with his wife and many children

in a hole near the river and the sound of the girl's weeping disturbed them. So he stuck one of his heads out of the hole and asked, "Why weep so loudly, child? You are disturbing my entire household, and we have new babies here."

"Oh, Father Cobra, please excuse me, but my stepmother has sold me to the Fish Prince and tomorrow he shall surely devour me for I hear he is very large and fierce."

"Listen, child, for I am very wise and know all things," said the seven-headed cobra. "This great fish is no ordinary fish but a rajah of a far-off country who has in some way offended the gods and as a punishment was turned into a fish. Do exactly as I say, and you can break the enchantment. But if you do not, surely he will eat you and spit out the little bones."

She nodded, no longer weeping, though tears still seeped from her eyes.

The snake disappeared for a moment into his hole, then reappeared with three stones. "Take these and keep them safe. When you are put in the little house next to the Fish Prince's tank, take care you do not fall asleep, no matter how tired you are. Watch until the fish comes up to speak. Throw the first stone at him and he will immediately sink down to the bottom of his tank. When next he surfaces, throw the second stone. He will go away again, but return a third time. Then you must throw the last stone at him and the enchantment will be broken. Can you remember all this?"

She nodded, and the rest of her tears dried up. Thanking him, she curtsied, and tied the three stones in the corner of her bridal sari. Then she ran back home where her stepmother was surprised to see how happy she had become.

•••

The next morning, as promised, the messengers came with the gold mohurs and left with Balna, and she went with them willingly, which distressed her stepmother even more.

The Ranee was waiting for her in the garden. When she saw how lovely and unafraid Balna was, the Ranee clapped her hands with joy. Then she led the girl to the little house and left her there.

"Be kind to my son, Prince Fish," the Ranee said.

Balna nodded, and the Ranee left.

Balna sat the rest of the day in the little house, eating fresh figs and rice that had been left for her, but she heard not a sound from the tank next door.

Day went and night came, and Balna was careful not to lie down or to fall asleep, but fingered the three smooth stones the cobra had given her.

At last it was midnight and strange sounds came from the tank. Waves dashed against the stone wall and a strong hissing sound, like steam, rose up from the water. Muchie Rajah rushed to the short wall, his mouth open and his scales glimmering red.

Balna was terribly frightened, but she held fast to the first stone and when the Fish Prince was close enough, she threw it at him. He caught the stone in his terrible mouth, closed his mouth, and sank immediately to the bottom of the tank.

But in minutes he had recovered and was once again rising up hissing like steam, his mouth open, his scales red as rubies.

Balna threw the second stone and a second time the Fish Prince swallowed the stone and dropped to the bottom of the tank.

It was a long time before he rose again, but this time when he rushed the wall, the water swamped over and wet Balna's feet. The Fish Prince's mouth was wide and she could see his sharp teeth. His scales were the color of blood.

She threw the last stone. No sooner did he close his mouth on it, then—just as the cobra had said—his enchantment was over. Instead of a great fish, there stood a handsome young rajah knee deep in the water. His turban was fastened with the three smooth stones that, when she got closer, Balna realized were really pearls.

The rajah smiled. "You have saved both my life and yours. If you will do me the honor of becoming my bride, we will live happily ever after. You are not only beautiful and brave, you are resourceful as well. I could not ask for more."

So they were married amid much splendor and feasting and for several months were deliriously happy.

But when the wicked stepmother heard of Balna's good fortune, she gnashed her teeth, determined that she would have that fortune for her own daughter. Hiding her wicked intentions behind smiles, she and her daughter went to the palace.

In her great joy, Balna forgave the woman all her past sins, and went walking with her stepmother and sister along the riverbank, innocently showing them her new rings and bracelets and crown.

"I have never seen so many jewels," said her stepsister, and Balna insisted the girl try them on.

No sooner had she given her stepsister the jewels, then stepmother and stepsister pushed her into the river and left her to drown. Then they hurried home.

The stepmother sent word to the palace that her daughter Balna had become terribly ill and could not see her new husband nor his mother or father for three weeks.

When the three weeks were up, the Muchie Rajah and the Rajah and the Ranee all came to take Balna home. How distressed they were when they saw the stepsister dressed in Balna's jewels. How coarse, ugly, and stupid the illness had left her.

But they took her back to the palace anyway. It never occurred to any of them that she was anyone other than Balna.

Now while the stepmother and the stepsister were enjoying their new luxuries, Balna was not dead. She had struggled in the water and had been saved— at the last moment—by the same seven-headed cobra who had given her the stones. He tended her for three weeks until she was quite recovered.

"Thank you very much," she said, "for you have saved me twice. But now I must go back for my Fish Prince must be worrying about me."

"If you go back now," said the cobra's wife, "your stepmother and stepsister will surely do you harm. Besides, I can see you are going to have a baby. I am very good with babies as you know."

"Listen to my good wife," said the cobra, "and wait until your prince comes looking for you."

So Balna stayed with the cobras, and gave birth months later to a beautiful child she named Muchie Lal, the Ruby Fish.

The cobras loved the little boy as if he were their own, for their own children had moved off to start their own families.

One day the seven-headed cobra met a bangle-seller whom he gave diamonds and rubies and pearls, saying, "Take these and make them into bangles for the little prince who lives with me whose name is Muchie Lal. There will be a handsome reward for you if you do it well. Bring the bangles to my hole by the side of the river."

So the bangle-seller did as he was instructed and was carrying the handsome bangles back to the river when he was met by Prince Fish who was out riding, as much to get away from his hideous wife as to have sport. Prince Fish was quite taken with the bangles but the seller would not let him have them.

"They belong to the old seven-headed cobra who lives in a

hole by the river. They are for a little prince who lives with him by the name of Muchie Lal."

This intrigued the Fish Prince. "Let me go in your place," he said. "And I will pay you what the old cobra owes." He gave the bangle-seller an entire purse filled with gold.

When Prince Fish arrived at the hole, carrying the bangles, little Muchie Lal ran out of the hole on his little legs, crying, "Bangles, bangles, are those for me?"

Muchie Lal was so exactly like his mother, the beautiful Balna, that the Fish Prince was taken aback. He held the bangles out. "You may have these, child, only first tell me your name and the name of your mother."

"My name is Muchie Lal and my mother is Ranee Balna and we live here with the seven-headed cobra and his wife. May I now have the bangles?" the boy asked, surprised that the handsome man before him had suddenly burst into tears.

Then out of the hole came Balna and after her the two cobras. And what a wonderful reunion that was, for the cobra had been a friend of the prince's when he'd been a fish in the river, which is how the cobra had known so much about him.

So they all went back to the palace and there was great outcry. Only when the stepmother and the fake ranee heard the sound of rejoicing and looked from the window and saw the true Balna, they were so afraid, they ran out the back way and got lost in the forest and were never heard from again.

◦

Spirits of the Wells

Folklorist R. P. Masani discovered, when he was Municipal Secretary of Bombay in the early 1900s, and tried to close down certain wells because of the threat of malaria, that many people still believed in spirits of the wells, a belief that ran at least back to the seventh century AD when some of the more ornate wells had been built.

•••

In 1560, it was reported that a fisherman in Ceylon caught seven mermen off the coast and when they were dissected, they had skeletons resembling a man's.

Chapter 6

MERMEN OF THE MIDDLE EAST

The Middle East was the place where legends of the great mer gods first arose. Dagon, the Phoenician fish-tailed god of the sea, was human from the waist up, fish below.

Ea-Enki, the Sumerian god of the earth downward, was sometimes depicted as a man with a fish body. He lived in the deep, sweet waters and was the god of the great Babylonian flood epic that pre-dated the Biblical flood story.

In one form, the god Osiris was the River Nile, both the river itself and the serpent/soul of the Nile. He was also the ocean into which the Nile flowed, as well as the great leviathan of the deep. The annual ritual of Osiris' death meant that the river could become fertile and renewed.

Hopo was also a god of the Nile. He carried a lotus on his head and was always depicted as pouring sacred waters from a vase.

And in the great collection, *The Thousand and One Nights*, more commonly called *The Arabian Nights*, is one of the best known stories of a merman.

THE TALE OF ABDULLAH OF THE LAND AND ABDULLAH OF THE SEA
Arabian Nights

There was once a fisherman named Abdullah who had a wife and nine children. They were so poor, he owned nothing but his net.

One day, when she had given birth to their tenth child, the wife said, "Go in the name of Allah and with the luck of our newborn, cast your net."

So Abdullah went out, cast his net, and caught nothing. The poor man's heart ached so, that when he went past the baker's shop, the smell of fresh bread left him near to fainting.

Seeing his friend so weak, the baker called out, "Good Abdullah, I will give you bread till you have luck again."

The fisherman was so grateful, he insisted the baker take his net in exchange, but the kind man would have none of it.

"Your net is your shop as the oven is mine," he said, putting the hot loaves in Abdullah's creel.

That night the fisherman's wife cried, "Allah is bountiful," and laid the loaves before her famished children.

•••

The next day, when it came time to draw in his net, Abdullah found it so heavy, his hands bled as he pulled it in. And wonder of wonders! There was a man caught in it.

"Mercy, oh Afrit of Solomon, oh Genie!" he cried.

"Do not be afraid, fisherman, I am as human as you, only I am one of the children of the sea. We, too, obey Allah's commandments. Set me free and whenever you call, 'Abdullah, O Merman,' I shall come to this place. Bring me grapes and figs and dates and pomegranates, and in return I shall fill your fishing basket with all manner of precious stones."

And so it was, fruit in exchange for jewels.

Abdullah's wife cautioned him to tell no one of their good fortune, but he answered, "I shall only tell the baker, who in my darkest hour had compassion upon me."

But the baker was not as circumspect as his friend, and the secret was told and retold.

•••

Now it seems that at that same time the queen's necklace of precious stones had been stolen and because Abdullah the fisherman suddenly had handfuls of jewels, he was arrested as a thief.

But just as he was taken before the king, the queen found her necklace. So the king got the fishermen to tell him the story of his covenant with Abdullah the merman.

The king was so impressed, he married his daughter to Abdullah as his second wife and established the fisherman's first wife and children in the palace. Then he made Abdullah his minister of the right hand, and the baker his advisor of the left hand.

•••

One day, as Abdullah of the Land and Abdullah of the Sea were conversing on the shore, the merman asked, "Would you care to see the land where I abide?"

"With greatest pleasure," the fisherman replied.

"Then I must anoint your whole body with a fat taken from the Dandan, a fish of miraculous properties. With it you shall be able to breathe under the waves."

And so it was. Abdullah of the Land saw the underwater city where only women who were not to conceive children lived, as well as cities where there were males and females together, and many children, and a sultan to rule over them. They all had human forms except that they had tails like fishes. Abdullah of the Land was astonished by what he saw. "The marvels of the sea are truly more manifold than the marvels of the land," he said.

Finally they came to a house of coral and pearl and emerald and there the fisherman met the merman's wife and daughter, both fair as the moon with tiny waists and black eyes and hair like spun gold.

"Oh father," the daughter cried, "is this the No-tail of whom you speak so often?" Then she and her mother began to laugh. The fisherman felt himself the brunt of a joke and was ashamed.

"Silence!" the merman cried, seeing his friend embarrassed, adding, "Forgive them. They have no wits."

Presently ten of the sultan's men arrived. "Have you a No-tail here?"

"This is he," the merman said, putting his arm around his friend. "I was just returning him to the land."

"We must take him to the sultan," they said, carrying Abdullah off to the sultan who spoke with him and agreed he must be returned at once.

The merman then handed the fisherman a purse to lay on the tomb of the prophet.

"I will," the fisherman promised.

But on the way back they came upon a group of mer-creatures singing and dancing.

"What is happening?" asked Abdullah of the Land.

"One of us has died," the merman said.

"Do you mean that when someone dies, you rejoice?"

"We do. And what do you do, you of the land?"

Abdullah shook his head. "We sorrow."

The merman stared at his friend in disbelief. "Give me back my purse," he cried. "I will have nothing to do with one who weeps when Allah takes what is his." And he tossed the fisherman onto the land and disappeared back under the waves.

From that time on, though the fisherman often went to the shore and called out for his comrade, the merman was never seen again.

Glory be to the Living whose Empire is of the Seen and the Unseen!

∼

Water Genii

In Morocco, there was a common belief that water genii lived in all the pools and ponds and rivers where they danced and made music. Often they played various instruments to keep themselves awake. Most of them were female, but a few were male.

If a child stumbled into the water, a gift had to be offered immediately to the genii. The child was given a mouthful of oil and spit it out at the spot in which he fell. And egg was also given to the child to throw into the water as another gift. All this was done to keep the genii from making the child fall ill.

Certain water genii made themselves visible to humans. Chief among these was Hamu Ukaiou and his wife, Aicha Kandida. Out of pure hatred for the human race, they killed whoever came into their reaches. He struck at women, his wife at men. But the smart traveler always sharpened a knife on the ground and this put both genii to flight.

Men of the Marshes

These were also genii—all male—who lived in the marshes around Marrakesh. Long after the marshes were drained, people still believed in the genii there.

Local women used to make pilgrimages on the twenty-seventh day of Ramadan to a large fountain called Riad Larouss in Marrakesh, where the marshes used to be. They would carry small clay vessels called *darraja*. These clay jars, once used for cosmetics, were filled with oil and incense and with a cotton wick, made usable lamps. The women would beg for good health from the men of the marshes, then leave the lamps at the fountain.

THE RIVER MONSTER
Persia/Iran

Once a terrible monster lived in the Persian rivers. He was so horrible to look at that the priests were convinced he had the power to flood the land. So they made sacrifices to him.

Now the rain god who lived in the sky was angry that the priests believed such nonsense. He was jealous, too, for it was he who actually caused floods. So he descended to the riverside, clad in wind, rain, and hail, to do battle with the monster.

They warred for days, and, suddenly, with a great swipe of his awful claws, the monster tore out the rain god's eyes. The rain god raced back to his home and sat in a sulfurous stink while he tried to figure out what to do.

At last he consulted a seer.

"Go back to earth and marry a mortal woman," said the seer. "She will help you get your eyes back."

This the rain god did, and he was led into the village by one of the local boys. Of course, blind as he was, he was not a particularly appealing bridegroom, but his great wealth and power spoke for him. He got himself a bride who was poor but beautiful.

Taking his bride back up into the skies, the rain god did what he could to make her happy. In turn, the girl worked hard at being a good wife.

One day, the rain god's wife asked, "What is there I can do to help you, my lord?"

He smiled. "You can help me get my eyes back from the monster who took them."

She bowed her head and was silent, but he could hear the fear in her movements. "Whatever you wish, husband," she said.

The very next day she went down to the riverbank and started combing her hair and singing. Soon the monster rose to the surface and stared at her. She was very beautiful and she did not run screaming when he appeared. Instead she looked at him, smiled, and opened her arms.

The monster was overcome with love, for no woman had ever smiled at him before. He lay down beside her, his hideous head in her lap, and she combed his horrible hair.

Finally he asked, "What can I give you, my love? What jewels to match your eyes, or gold to wear on your breast?" For the priests had showered even more gifts on him since he had defeated the rain god.

"No gold or jewels," she said, in a voice soft as doom. "All I want are the eyes of the rain god to wear in my hair."

Of course he went immediately and fetched them for her. She put them like pearls in her hair and then sang him to sleep.

As soon as the monster was snoring, she rose and went back up to the sky. She placed the eyes in her husband's empty sockets and at once he could see again.

Did he say how beautiful she was? Did he praise her courage?

No—he ran right back down to the riverside where he found the monster still asleep.

"Wake up, you sleeping abomination!" he cried, and when the monster woke, they battled once again, only this time the rain god won. He killed the beast, chopped off its head, and brought that awful burden up to his wife as a gift.

Horrified, the wife dropped the terrible present and flung herself over the side of the sky into the river below, where she drowned.

～

Pliny, in his *Natural History*, reported that when Mena was president of Egypt and was walking along the banks of the Nile, he encountered a merman, "a Sea-monster in the shape of a man" with yellow hair intermixt with gray, who came out of the water. According to Pliny, the seaman looked like a man up to his middle, but "his other parts ended in a fish."

Chapter 7

MERMEN OF AFRICA

The countries in Africa are many and over a thousand different languages are spoken there. The religious beliefs are varied, too, though most of the old belief-systems crumbled under the colonial occupations. However the stories and tales told still hold vivid sway over the imagination of the people.

For a long time, the only tale-collecting done on the African continent was, in folklorist Richard Dorson's words, "gathered…and published by missionaries, travelers, administrators, linguists, and anthropologists incidentally to their main pursuits." In fact no major folklore work was done there prior to the 1960s.

Africa is an ocean-girt continent, though not all of its countries touch the ocean. But some of the great rivers of the world—like the Nile (see also the chapter on the Mermen of the Middle East)—can be found there. And where there are large river systems, there always seem to be tales of water spirits, water demons, merfolk. There are also water gods, like Libanza who lives in a misty region below the Congo River, and Kianda who is the Angolan Neptune.

Dogir

In the northern Sudan, the Nubian people used to believe in the dogir, spirits who lived in the Nile River. The dogir had such a well-ordered society, they even paid taxes!

Sometimes a dogir man came ashore and, finding a human woman bathing in the shallows, carried her off as his wife. From this belief grew the custom of allowing women to wash clothes in the river but not to bathe there. Even as late as the 1950s, this belief lingered. A story reported by Jan Knappert in *African Mythology*, tells of a woman near the town of Umbarakab who claimed to have a dogir lover visiting her at night in the shape of a little man.

Farther south, the dogir were not seen as being so friendly, but rather were thought to be devourers of human flesh.

Hydra
In Mali the Fulani people believed in a water monster called Hydra, or Waterlord, to whom they brought offerings so that it would not stop the river's flow.

THE GIRL AND THE WATERLORD
Mali

There was once a pregnant woman, second wife to a man whose other wife teased her most unmercifully. She went down to the river, and sang to the Waterlord,

> My co-wife troubles me,
> She fills my water jar with mud,
> She takes my place at my husband's side.
> If you will help me,
> The child I carry in my belly even now
> Shall be yours.

The Waterlord heard her and rose from the river and gave her aid, cleaning the jar and even placing it back on her head.

That very night she gave birth to a little daughter whom she called Jinde Sirinde, or the One for the Waterlord.

And the co-wife never bothered the woman again.

•••

Now when Jinde Sirinde was old enough to bring water from

the river on her own, she was one day cleaning her jar, standing in the river up to her knees. The Waterlord saw her and remembered that she was his, and he drew her down to the deepest part of the river to be his wife.

"For your mother gave you to me the day you were born," he told Jinde Sirinde.

"Please, my lord," said Jinde Sirinde, "may I go ashore one last time to say goodbye to my mother?"

"You may have one day," said the Waterlord. "Then you must return. A woman belongs to her husband. If you do not come back by nightfall, I shall come ashore and take you."

Jinde Sirinde swam up to the surface before he could change his mind, and then ran to her mother's house.

But her mother was frightened and would not open the door. And her father was frightened. And the co-wife was frightened, too.

So Jinde Sirinde went to the boy she loved and who loved her. "The Waterlord wants me as his bride and he will come for me tonight if I do not go back into the river," she said.

This boy took his father's old sword. "I will fight for you," he said. "Stay here with me and we will be married."

So she stayed and that night the Waterlord rose up from the river like a storm. He raced across the fields. When he came into the village, he was a hydra, with scaly skins and seven heads.

"Where is Jinde Sirinde?" he roared. "She who was promised to me."

"Jinde is my wife now," said her lover. With the old sword, he slashed off all seven of the hydra's heads, one at a time.

And so Jinde Sirinde did not have to marry the Waterlord after all.

~

Olokun

This is the Nigerian God of Waters and the Deep, the most worshipped god in the Benin kingdom. Synonymous with the oceans of the earth, he provided humans with goods, health, and women.

In the Benin pantheon, Olokun represented purity, luck, happiness, and he was most often depicted as walking about on two enormous mudfish, carrying a lizard in each hand.

Nommos

The Dogon, a West African tribe of (possibly) Egyptian descent believed that awful-looking beings called nommos came from Sirius, the dog star, and settled under the sea. It was from the nommos that the Dogon—so it is said—learned their knowledge of the heavens.

Kianda

The Angolan god of the Atlantic Ocean and all the fish. He lived in an underwater palace.

KIANDA TAKES A BRIDE
Angola

Kianda the god was lonely so he came out of the ocean in the shape of a skull.

Two sisters were walking along the shore, and Kianda in his skull voice asked the eldest to be his bride.

She took up a stick. Bam! Bam! She hit the skull. She did not want to marry him.

He flew over to the younger sister who received him with great courtesy. She gave him food. She accepted his proposal.

"Follow me," the skull said, and the younger sister went after him.

He flew to a rock wall where a door opened, and in they went. It turned into a huge palace. Servants came to greet her, calling out, "Here is the queen! Here is the queen."

Then her husband took off his skull disguise and he was handsome as a god.

"I am Kianda," he told her. "You will rule the ocean with me."

They had many children, who had human figures but could breath underwater just like fish.

As for the eldest sister who had been so discourteous, she married a kishi, a man-eating demon who came to her in the shape of a handsome man. After she gave birth to a child with two faces—one hyena and one human—the kishi devoured her.

~

Water People

In Liberia, the Kpelle people believed that in their rivers lived people with human heads but fish abdomens. In the mornings, these long-haired spirits would sit on rocks, sunning themselves. If you asked them for money, they would give it to you—but at a price. Supposedly the water people's request was: "Only if you bring us a white ram every month, a length of white cloth, and your wife or mother or daughter, can we make you rich."

Njuzu

In Zimbabwe, the water sprites are called njuzu and they are the guardians of pure water. They may appear as fish with a human head. Born in mountain caves where the springs of rivers first arise, they abhor loud noises. The people of Zimbabwe say that when the Europeans came with their noisy machines, many njuzu left their streams and rivers forever— which is why so many have dried up.

Chapter 8

MERMEN OF THE PACIFIC ISLANDS

The Polynesian and Austronesian people were great sailors and their small island nations were completely surrounded by water. So it is not surprising that they peopled their mythic pantheons with many sea gods, water spirits, water demons, et cetera. Many of their beliefs centered more often around goddesses than gods. Here are some of the mermen in their cosmology.

Tangaroa
The Maori god of the waters, all the fish were his children.

In-Guas
Australian Aboriginal water spirit who drowns people in his pool.

Tirnivan and Vatea
Brother gods of the Hervey Islands, Vatea was half man and half shark. He was the inventor of nets and fishing. His brother, Tirnivan, was lord of all the fish. He was half man and half sprat.

Ponaturi
These Maori sea fairies who are Pacific Ocean spirits (and sometimes ogres) come in both male and female forms. In most of the stories, they are at war with the great Maori heroes.

HOW RUA-PUPUKE FOUND HIS SON
Maori

Rua-Pupuke had one son who went out swimming with his friends one day and sank. The boys ran home to tell his father.

"Show me this place," said Rua-Pupuke, for he guessed that the sea fairies had taken his son.

The boys took him to the spot where the boy had disappeared.

"Go tell my wife to wait for me here," Rua-Pupuke told the boys. As soon as they had left, he turned himself into a great fish, a whale, and swam down to the palace of the Sea King, which was built of human bones.

Rua-Pupuke looked at the carved bones. There over the lintel of the door he recognized his son.

"Father!" the boy cried, because he knew his father, even in his fish shape.

Rua-Pupuke took the boy's bones in his mouth and swam back up to the beach. There he spit the boy out in his whole form, and the boy ran into his mother's waiting arms.

Rua-Pupuke came onto the shore and turned back into a man. He sent the boy to a secret place in the woods to hide, because once the Sea King had a soul, he never let it go.

Then Rua-Pupuke found an old house and fixed it so that not a single ray of light shone in.

That night, up to the old house, came a company of people, but Rua-Pupuke knew it was the Sea King's company in disguise searching for his son.

Rua-Pupuke bowed and led them into the house and ordered cooks to make a great meal for them. He said nothing of his son. They ate and ate until they were so sleepy, they had to retire.

The house was dark and they did not know when day had come, so they kept sleeping. Rua-Pupuke ordered his men to set fire to the house, and they burned it to the ground.

The spirits had nowhere else to go, their human bodies having been burned, so they flew back into the sea and did not bother Rua-Pupuke or his son again.

Adaro

A Solomon Islands sea spirit who was a man with tail fins on his feet, gills behind his ears. He also had a shark's fin made of horn on his back and on his head a long pike, like a swordfish. Not only did he swim in the sea, he could travel along the rainbow and kill people by shooting poisonous flying fish.

Aremata-Rorua and Aremata-Popoa

Also known as "Long Wave" and "Short Wave," these two ocean demons were the ones most feared by the famed Polynesian mariners.

Lumakaka

This was a Papuan sea giant who was a devourer of people.

THE SEA GIANT
Papua

Once an old man and his grandsons lived by the water and made their living fishing.

It was on a clouded-over day that the grandfather decided to stay at home, and only the boys went out. But when their boat was full of all kinds of fish, the silver fins shining, Lumakaka appeared, rising up out of the water like a mountain.

"I am hungry!" he roared.

The boys did not hesitate. They threw him a fish, and he disappeared back down into his watery home. Knowing the giant would not be satisfied for long, the boys started to paddle for home.

Sure enough, the giant once again rose up out of the waves. "I am still hungry!" he roared.

They threw fish after fish at him, and still he wanted more.

And they were so far from home.

"What shall we do, brother?" cried the elder. "There are no more fish and now he will devour us, too."

"Quick!" the younger brother said. "Cut off my arm."

The elder brother cut off the younger's arm and flung it into the sea. Lumakaka caught the arm, ate it, and asked for more.

The younger brother's second arm was thrown to the giant and now, when Lumakaka disappeared beneath the waves, the elder brother had to paddle on his own.

Soon the younger brother's legs went the way of his arms. Then his trunk. But at last the boat touched land and the elder brother tenderly carried what was left into the house.

"Let us bury Brother's head," said grandfather. "It will grow into a magic coconut tree and feed us for the rest of our lives."

So they did this, and what the grandfather said came true, and they never had to go to the sea again.

~

Kyai Blorong

An East Javanese fish-tailed servant of the sea goddess, also known as Kyai Belorong, he had one thousand arms and legs and a fish tail. Covered with scales, he ruled over the mermaids who were his servants. His palace was situated on the sea bed, with a roof made of skeletons. Living men were the pillars of his house, punishment for their excessive greed.

Kyai Blorong owned gold without limits and anyone wishing to have some was allowed to take it away, on one condition: they would then have only seven more years to live.

Jin Laut

This Indonesian sea demon could kill someone simply by sitting on his chest. He was a servant of the Goddess of the Southern Ocean.

Machanu

In Thailand, Machanu was the half-man, half-fish guardian of the lake that all dead souls had to cross to get to the underworld.

Chapter 9

MERMEN OF THE NEW WORLD

The North and South American native peoples had distinct and varied culture heroes, animal stories, trickster tales, et cetera. Only a few of them dealt with water spirits, fewer still with mermen.

Also, after the shores of the Americas were visited by travelers from Europe and the Russias, not to mention possible Polynesian travelers, the Native American stories were infiltrated (some would say contaminated) with other cultural influences.

For example, the following tale from the Oregon Coast has interesting parallels with the Matthew Arnold poem and the Danish ballad of the forsaken merman. (*See* pages 17–18.)

THE WOMAN WHO MARRIED A MERMAN
Coos Indians

In the village of Takimaya on the Oregon Coast lived a girl and her five brothers. She was beautiful and a hard worker and many men wanted to marry her. But she was not willing to be married to any of them.

Now every day she liked to swim in a little creek near her home. One day on her way home from swimming, she suddenly found a stranger walking beside her. She had not heard him come up to her.

She did not speak to him, but he spoke to her. "I live in a village at the bottom of the sea," he said. "Many times I have watched you swimming and I have fallen in love with you. Will you return with me and be my wife?"

Now she was willing to be married. So she hung on to his belt and closed her eyes and he dove into the ocean. When she opened her eyes again, they were down at the bottom of the water and there was his village.

Her husband was one of five sons of the chief of the village, and for several years, they lived contented there.

The girl and the man from under the water had a son. When he became big enough, the woman taught him to shoot with bow and arrows that she made for him. When she put him to bed each night she would sing to him, and tell him of his five uncles on land.

"They have many arrows up there," she would say. "Much better than the ones I make down here. Up in the world of air, the arrows fly more swiftly and surely."

One day the boy asked to meet his land uncles.

"Only if your father says we may go," said his mother.

The father would not let both of them go, but at last he agreed that his wife might make a visit. When they had married, he had promised her she could see her brothers every now and then. She had never gone up above before.

So the next morning, dressed in five otter skins, she swam up to the world of air. But when her brothers saw her, they thought she was a real otter, and being great hunters, they shot at her and hit her again and again. But she did not get hurt. None of the arrows stayed in the otter fur.

At last they all gave up, except for the oldest brother. He followed the otter to a little beach where she took off her skins and there he recognized his long lost sister.

"Yes," she said, "I am the sea otter. I am married now, to a man from under the water. He is the son of a chief. I have come to get real arrows for our little boy to play with." She gave him the otter skins and he gave her as many more arrows as she could carry.

Just before she was ready to go back into the water, she said,

"Tomorrow on the beach near the village will be a whale. Divide it among the people. It is my husband's bride gift to you."

Several moons later she returned again to visit her brothers and they noticed that her shoulders were scaly and dark, like a serpent's. She stayed with them a little while, and then returned to the sea. They never saw her again.

But long afterwards, a family of sea serpents came to the shore, and the brothers shot arrows toward them so that they could gather the arrows. Every summer and every winter there were two whales stranded on the beach by the village, a gift from the family under the sea.

~

A few Native American creation stories include a man/god from under the sea. This is one from Wisconsin.

THE MAN WHO ROSE UP FROM THE SEA
Shawano Indians

Long ago, when the people lived in Asia, across the great land mass, they were hungry and cold for the land was hard and they could not find much to eat.

Then one day a man rose up from the sea and spoke to them. At least they thought he was a man, but instead of legs he had two tails, each one a fish. His face was like a porpoise's being pointed, and he had green hair that resembled seaweed.

Still, he spoke like a man, singing in a voice of the people: "Come to me, come below the waves, for there my people swim through the green light. There is no hunger here. No fear. Come, my brothers of the land. Come."

The people of the land talked among themselves, but they knew that no one who went into the sea returned.

The seaman understood this and sang. "Be not afraid my brothers, for beyond this Great Salt there lies another, where you and your wives and your children can live."

So then the people were not afraid. They built great boats and gathered up all that they owed. They followed the fish-man to America where they built their new homes and planted their seeds, and so flourished.

~

Kolowissi
This is a Zuni sea serpent who changes into a handsome man, and then marries a maiden who has—all by accident—bathed in his sacred pool. There is a quite similar story told in Guiana.

Unktahe
This Dakota water god is a wily sorcerer who could control both dreams and magic. He fought constantly with Waukheo, the Thunder-bird.

Water Manitou
An Ojibway water god with a silver tail, he liked to take beautiful women under the water.

Water Babies
These small beings who live in lakes, ponds, springs, rivers are feared by many different Native American groups, especially those who live around the Great Basin. Though not actual babies, these spirits include a mannikin who pulls at fishermen's lines.

Inue

Though the Inuit (Eskimo) people worshipped a sea goddess—Sedna—they also believed in Inue, who was a kind of merman. But on the sea bottom there were also occasionally other folk. This story, like many Inuit stories, is essentially bare-boned and unpleasant.

THE BOY FROM THE BOTTOM OF THE SEA
Greenland Inuits

An obstinate man took a wife and he beat her every day for no reason. Often she would try and run away to another house in the village, but her husband always found her and took her back. One day when he wanted to make a special point of the beating, he hit her with a wooden box.

So she ran away, for she was pregnant and feared losing the child. She walked straight into the sea but was not drowned. Instead she found herself in the bottom of the sea.

So she built herself a house of seaweed and old bones. And when she was there a few months, the child was born. He did not look like a human child. His eyes were jellyfish, his hair seaweed, and his mouth like a mussel.

The child grew and grew. When he was old enough, he heard children playing up on the land and said, "I want to go and see them."

"When you are stronger," said his mother.

So the sea boy began doing exercises with great stones, to get strong. At last he was strong enough.

He heard the children up above crying, "Iyoi-iyoi-iyoi."

"I will go now, mother," said the sea boy.

"I will go with you, for I have suffered much evil there. I will tell you where to go, and which house to visit. Be sure when you look in, you make an angry face."

So they went up and the boy started into one house.

"Not that one," cried his mother, "for when I was being beaten, they were good to me and took me in. Go that other house." She pointed to the place her husband lived.

Her son went to the house and pushed his face in through the door. All those who were inside fell down dead of fright. He would have beaten his father if he could, but his father had died long since. Then the boy went back down into the sea with his mother.

When the day dawned, the people in the one house saw tracks filled with seaweed leading up to the other house, but it was quiet in there.

They went inside and found all the people dead. So they followed the tracks back to the sea.

∽

Encantados

Along the Amazon River in South America, a distinction was drawn between the mermaids (*serias*), who were seen as a kind of fish, and the encantados, who were people in fish clothes. The serias were all female, but the encantados were both female and male and often referred to as dolphins, or *botos*.

The encantados lived in a city at the bottom of the river. Often botos took people down to the city where they, too, became encantados. Once someone ate or drank anything, they had to stay forever. If, however, they refrained from eating or drinking, they could still be rescued by a shaman/priest, a *sacaca*.

Sometimes a boto fell in love with a human woman and seduced her. Children often came from such unions. The botos were especially attracted by menstruating women. The only way to keep them away from the women at such a time was for the women to wear crosses of garlic and carry strands of chili peppers because those were thought to burn the noses of the predacious botos. Cigar smoke was also thought to be useful and many a sacaca smoked during his healing work. Also a knife drawn along the boat's side or in the water was believed to keep the botos away.

The botos were also said to have a sixth finger and a sixth sense that let them read human thoughts. They were also able to command the attention of humans, and lure them into the water.

If someone standing on the riverbank heard mysterious laughter or the wailing of a violin, he knew it was the encantados partying beneath the water.

"The person who kills a dolphin is always punished," goes one adage, as this story demonstrates.

THE WOUNDED DOLPHIN
Brazil

One November day, a fisherman harpooned a boto, a dolphin as wrinkled as an old man.

Suddenly nine botos came from all over and began chasing the fisherman, because the old one he had killed was their grandfather.

Try as he might, the fisherman could not escape the botos without killing them, too. Nine. He killed all nine.

After that he could not sleep. He tried setting up his mosquito net and lying down in his hammock. But nothing worked. He could not sleep. He had killed ten botos and when he closed his eyes, there was light all around him, bright as day. Any time he finally dozed off, some mysterious hands shook his hammock and he woke again.

His father finally had to call a sacaca to cure him. He was a real sacaca, too—one who could go down to the river bottom with a lighted cigarette and return with it still lit.

The sacaca came, heard the story, and shook his head. "Very bad," he said. "Not one but ten botos you killed. There is no help for it. Whenever it is November, you won't sleep right."

And so it was, every year in November, the fisherman could not sleep. Not a wink. For the rest of his life.

~

Sea Spirit
This was a sometimes malevolent mer god of the Mapuche people who are a branch of the Araucanian Indians who once inhabited much of the southern Andes (in Chile) and were never defeated by either the Incas or the Spanish. The sea spirit often took a human woman to be his bride. He could wreak terrible vengeance if thwarted in his desires.

RAYEN-CAVEN AND THE SEA SPIRIT
Chile

Once a poor fisherman named Curi-Caven lived by the side of the sea. He had a lovely daughter, Rayen-Caven, whose mother had died early in the spring.

Because Curi-Caven had to be out in his fishing boat all day long, the little girl had to raise herself. He was in great despair and whenever he was home, he would sit at the door of his cabin groaning about his fate.

One day the Sea Spirit came to his door. "If I train your daughter for you, teach her all of the womanly arts, will you grant a wish?"

Eagerly Curi-Caven agreed.

"When she is twenty," said the Sea Spirit, "she shall be my bride."

True to his promise, the Sea Spirit taught the girl everything she needed to know to be well educated in the womanly skills, though he never showed himself to her. She learned to do all the things a mother would have taught her: to sew, to spin, to weave, to cook, to clean. It was as if the air taught her.

Curi-Caven never told his daughter of his bargain. In fact as the years went by, he forgot it himself.

Then one day, when Rayen-Caven was past nineteen, she brought a young man home. His name was Necul-Narqui. Rayen-Caven told her father that they were in love and wished his blessing to marry.

Then Curi-Caven remembered. "But perhaps the Sea Spirit has forgotten," he told himself. "After all, we have not heard from him for many years."

But a week before Rayen-Caven turned twenty, a week before she was to marry, the Sea Spirit came to the house.

"I have come to claim my wife," he said. "In seven days we will be married. Prepare her for me." Then he was gone.

What could Curi-Caven do but call his daughter and her beloved to him and tell them all.

"I shall fight this spirit," cried Necul-Narqui. "For Rayen-Caven is meant to be my bride."

The day before the wedding, Curi-Caven went out fishing as usual. But when he was far from shore, he looked back over his left shoulder and saw a cloud scudding over the waves. It headed straight for shore, to the little hut where his daughter and her beloved were preparing for their wedding.

The storm gathered itself right above the little hut and slammed down on it. Sand whirled about and buried the entire village, with all the people. Only Curi-Caven out in his fishing boat was left alive to mourn.

～

Loa

Loas were Haitian spirits or deities who possessed people during religious rites. They lived under the water in a dry and airy place that looked somewhat like Haiti itself.

If a loa had children, he came to visit them by way of the water road.

Often people drawing water from a spring at night heard the voices of the loa, or the sound of their drumming.

Though not strictly mermen, they did live beneath the water.

Agwe Woyo

The sea god of the West Indies, Agwe Woyo was greeted by a strange ritual even into the late 1970s when it was reported that a boat, fully flagged, was sailed out into the sea. On the boat were a priest, several men, and several women. The priest held up two white chickens as the women fell to the deck in an ecstatic fervor. Next a sacrificial ram was pushed overboard. Finally, on a model ship built specially for the purpose, were piled the slaughtered chickens, a seven-tiered cake, and other ritual offerings. The men heaved the little boat overboard where it sank, a final offering to Agwe Yoyo. At that, the women stood up and everybody sang a great song of rejoicing.

•••

During the days of the South American colonies, mermen and mermaids were commonly "sighted" by Europeans posted there. One such was seen in the 1500s, near the great rock Diamon off the coast of Martinique. The person who sighted the merman gave a long, precise description to the notary, which he ended this way: "It wiped its face and blew its nose before diving under the waves."

Epilogue

And so the mermen swam through the misty seas of myth, legend, and folklore, both written and oral. At times he was fish-tailed and scaly, with green hair and iron teeth. At other times his body had a pearly luminescence, reflecting the coral halls of his palace. Sometimes he had legs, or fish fins, or fish feet, or the gray velvet fur of the seal. But always he made his home under the waters, too deep for anyone but the dreamers or the drowned.

There are still today people who claim to have seen such creatures. For example, the loa are worshipped in Haiti among the more rural folk. And Duncan Williamson, the extraordinary Scottish storyteller who grew up among the travelers, writes that his father used to play his bagpipes for the seals "and they would all pop their heads out of the water, stand up straight listening." His father—and the other travelers—believed in selchies, and treated them with the greatest respect.

Gordon Bok, the Maine folksinger, who is at much at home on sea as on land, wrote to us:

> I once worked with a man who I swear was a selchie—at least a seal-man. Wrote a story about him… But he wasn't from Maine. The "eastward" was about all I ever heard him saying, which at times could have meant anything East of Campobello.

Bok, like lorists and singers and balladeers before him, enriches the legendary world of mermen with his own believing. Like the formal storytellers of earlier societies— wandering minstrels, shamans, jongleurs, court poets, and the like—he entwines legend with fact.

•••

The merman swims in and out of formal literature as well. For example, James Joyce wrote of Manannan MacLir brooding on the hearth:

…and would be
A merman bold,
Sitting lone
Under the sea
With a crown of gold
On a throne?

Matthew Arnold, John Milton, Thomas Campion, Henry Wadsworth Longfellow, and other poets took the merman as their own. Fantasists such as L. Frank Baum (who wrote the Oz books), E. Nesbit, Hans Christian Andersen, and the authors of this book, to name a few, have put mermen and sea gods in their stories.

Tritons decorate the statuary on the pathway to New York City's Rockefeller Center and caper around the fountains in the Bronx Zoo. The French Romanesque churches of Candes St Martin, Vezelay, and Cunault, among many, sport mermen atop their columns. On a wrought-iron gate surrounding the Queen's House in Greenwich, England, is a merman, crowned and mustached. This same merman, with his twin, guards the Naval Hospital at Greenwich. Mermen decorate the metalwork on a Bavarian hunting rifle of the seventeenth century, a suit of armor for a horse and man of the fifteenth century, and a harpsichord made in 1600—all on display at the Metropolitan Museum of Art in New York City. Such art objects and many more found around the world attest to the hidden popularity of mermen.

There is inescapable irony here. Once, we simply reaped the sea and populated it with our dream creatures. Now we are raping the sea, plowing poison into the sea lanes, or ruthlessly hunting to the brink of extinction many of the sea creatures who were the origins of these dreams: seal, whale, dugong, walrus, dolphin, porpoise, manatee. It is, in a way, an ultimate denial of these great old legends.

But think of this: it is more than likely—as our lands are overpopulated, our air made unbreathable—that we turn to the sea again for food, for shelter, for energy, for survival. To save ourselves from extinction. And as we do, who knows...

Those old dreams may well become our new reality. With gene manipulation, we may develop webbed feet, fingers joined by a fragile strand of transparent skin, our lungs linked to gill slits, a nictitating membrane guarding our eyes. In other words, we may become what our imaginations have desired since the childhood of the world: Merfolk swimming through crystal palaces set in sands of luminescent gold.

Glossary of the Gods of the Sea

There were many hundreds of sea gods. This glossary deals with the main ones only.

Aegir (Norse): a *jotunn* or personification of nature, chief among the sea giants. Also called Hler ("sheltered") or Gymir ("concealer"). Brother to Kari of air and Loki of fire. Pictured with long, white beard, thin, scraggly white hair, and claw-like, convulsing fingers, Aegir lived in a coral palace on the ocean bottom with his wife Ran. They dwelled among booty from wrecked ships. There they held great feasts and Aegir was admiringly called "Ale Brewer."

In this underwater castle, Aegir was served by Elde and Funfeng, the phosphorescence of the sea, as well as his nine beautiful daughters, the Billow Maidens.

The ocean is called "Aegir's brewing kettle" or "Aegir's Vat." Rivers are known as "Aegir's doors."

Agwe or **Agwe Woyo** (Haitian): the Voodoo sea god. His emblems were shells, oars painted blue or green, miniature boats. A mulatto, fair of skin and green-eyed, he dressed in the uniform of a naval officer, wearing a helmet and carrying white gloves. Blue and white were his sacred colors. He was said to be responsible for thunder over the ocean, the sound of his canons shooting.

Lasting through the twentieth century, a sacrifice ritual to Agwe was performed on a brightly-flagged boat.

Ahti (Finnish): Also known as Ahto. Pictured as an old bearded man living under the sea with his generous wife Vellamo. They raised a brood of water sprites.

Beher (Ethiopian): The sea god of Ethiopia, Beher is part of a triumvirate of gods—including Astar and Mahrem—but he is the leader of the three.

Chiccan (Mayan): This group of rain gods lived deep underwater in a lake.

Dagon (Phoenician): Called "fish-tailed god of the sea," though some also referred to him as the god of the corn. Pictured as human from waist up, fish below, he was sometimes confused with Ea-Enki.

Deva (Indian): Originally one of the ocean gods whose name—say some scholars—and attributes became transformed into the British/American idea of Davy Jones' locker, which is where drowned souls go.

Dragon Kings of the Sea (Chinese): Covered with scales, walking on four feet, able to leap into the sky to bring the rain, the dragon kings usually changed into human form when they dealt with humans. Beaten in a fight or slain, they often became dragons once again. As humans, they were fat little men with long beards, heavy mustaches, enormous eyebrows. There were four of them—for the four seas that supposedly surround the earth. The leader was Lung-Wang.

Ea-Enki (Sumerian): He was Lord of the Earth downward, and considered the wisest of the gods, all knowing. Arising from the Persian Gulf, he was worshipped at Eridu as the source of all wisdom. Sometimes he was depicted as a man in a fish body, sometimes as completely human. Living in the deep sweet-waters, his birth was recounted in the Babylonian epic *Enuna-Elish*. He was the god of the flood in the great Babylonian myth that predates the Biblical flood story.

Fe'e (Samoan): War god who was a great octopus under the sea. His tentacles reached into the far corners of the world and his voice could be heard in the thunder. He lived in an undersea palace called Bale-Fe'e.

Glaukos (Greek): Not originally a god, he was a human fisherman who found an herb of everlasting life in the sea. When he ate it, he leaped into the sea and was transformed into a sea god.

Hapi (Egyptian): God of the Nile, he was fat, bearded, with the body of a man but the breasts of a woman to prove his fertility. He carried a lotus on his head and poured sacred waters from a vase.

Hopo (Chinese): The most famous Chinese river god who demanded the sacrifice of young girls of royal blood. He was also called Count of the River.

Hu (Dahoman): A shark god who demanded human sacrifice. Each year his worshippers dressed the chosen man in a noble's clothes, carried him by hammock to the harbor, rowed him out to sea, and threw him overboard.

Ika-Tere (Polynesian): Father of the fish, he was the grandson of the ocean god, Tangaroa. He sired all the fish in the ocean and was their wise ruler. Some of his children were mermen and mermaids, though oddly their right sides were fish, while their lefts were human.

Jamm (Ugaritic): Once the water and sea god of the Ugarits, "Lord River" was later a water god of the Phoenicians. Ambitious and vain, he fought continually with the other gods. He was pictured both as a man and a sea monster.

Kala (Javanese): The ocean god of Java.

Kalunga (Brazilian): The sea god in Bahia, Brazil, where the Congo-Angola cult still holds sway.

Kane-Hoalani (Polynesian): Father of the Hawaiian goddess Pele, Kane owned a tiny magical seashell that if placed on the ocean would grow into an enormous sailing ship with sails the color of mother of pearl. Anyone climbing on board needed only say the name of his destination, and the ship would carry him there in the blink of an eye.

Khnum (Egyptian): Also known as Num, Khnemu, and Kneph, he was the god of the world-ocean and creator of man who sometimes appeared as a serpent. His consort was Heqet, frog-headed goddess in charge of resurrecting human. Sacred boats were dedicated to him and festivals in his name were held on the Egyptian rivers.

Kianda (Angolan): This Angolan god ruled the Atlantic Ocean and all the fish in its waters. He appeared on earth occasionally as a skull. His underwater home was a palace where he was taken care of by many servants.

Kompira (Japanese): This ugly, big-bellied sea god who sat cross-legged under the waves was at one time the most popular god in Japan. Once a demon, he was won over to Buddhism and became the god of happiness.

He was the sailor's god whose main shrine is in the village of Kotohira. At one time nearly all Japanese ships carried a charm from his shrine. To his great shrine come thousands of pilgrims yearly, especially on October 10th, his festival day. There they receive an amulet with the character "gold" engraved on it, for Kompira is also the god of prosperity who is often pictured carrying a purse.

In the nineteenth century, sailors aboard warships used to throw small casks of coins overboard when passing Kompira's shrine. Some modern fishermen pray to Kompira to end the chemical pollution of Japan's waters.

Korshid (Kurdish): This ruler of the sea is pictured as riding a mighty horse named Rawan ("son of the sea") that can run for six months without stopping.

Libanza (Bangalan/Zairean): One of two principal Bangala gods, Libanza lived with his sister-wife Nsongo below the waters of the Congo River. He traveled easily along the water route and because he controlled its levels, he meted out punishment or reward to the people who lived along its banks. His was an opulent kingdom, so the Bangala people hoped that when they died, they would go there.

Lir (Irish): The Irish sea god, also called Lear, whose son Manannan overtook his fame.

Mambang Tali Harus (Malaysian): The ruler of the sea from the mid-currents on the Malay peninsula, Bali, Java, and Sumatra.

Manannan Maclir (Irish): Also known as Manawyddan, this shapeshifting sea god was the son of Lir. Always dressed in green, he was blue-eyed and golden-haired like all the De Danann, the Irish elven folk.

Manannan owned a number of magical possessions: a coracle called "Wave Sweeper" that read the mind of its master and went where he willed; a cloak of invisibility called "Feth Faida" that looked like sea mist; a mighty sword, "Fragarach" ("Answerer"), that could cut through any armor and never failed to slay; a horse, "Splendid Mane," that could ride over sea and land with equal ease. He also owned a golden cup, which if three lies were told over it, would break in three. But if three truths were spoken over it, the cup would become whole again. There was a chalice that was never empty of drink and enchanted pigs that, once eaten, sprang to life again.

Manannan invented a spell that allowed a sorcerer to transform anyone into any shape. He was also keeper of a stronghold shaped like a beehive called "Oeth and Anoeth," which was made out of human bones.

Besides being king of the sea, Manannan was also a magician king and a sturdy protector of Ireland. But slowly power was taken from him. First his wife Fann, the "Pearl of Beauty," fell in love with the mortal hero Cuchulain. Though she eventually returned to her husband, it was a signal of the end. When Christianity came to Ireland, Manannan abdicated his underwater throne in AD 563 and moved to the Isle of Man, where he was worshipped into the beginning of the twentieth century. The Manx coat of arms—three legs forming a wheel—is said to be the shape in which Manannan rolled across the island.

Mimir (Norse): Son of Aegir, he was a giant who became known as the god of the primeval ocean or open sea. He lived in Mimir's Well, right next to the roots of the world-tree, Yggdrasil. Wiser than anyone in the world, having drunk from the well, he had future knowledge as well as past. Only once did he let someone else drink from his well of wisdom—the god, Odin. In exchange, Odin gave Mimir one of his eyes.

Mbomba (Zairean): Also known as Sangu, this huge water-monster is a river god and king of frogs and fish. Fishermen used to bring offerings to him before starting out.

Nav (English): The god of the waters from whom the word "navy" comes.

Ndauthina (Fijian): The god of fishermen and all seafarers, Ndauthina's name means "torch bearer." He is known as a seducer of women.

Neptune (Roman): Neither as popular as the Japanese Kompira nor as powerful as the Greek Poseidon from whom most of his attributes come, Neptune was considered a breeder of horses who created the very first horse. His own steeds were bronze-hoofed and golden-maned. When he rode, the sea before him turned smooth and great sea monsters gamboled in his path. The first mention of Neptune in either the annals or poetry came in 399 BC when a festival was ordained for him. In the second century BC, the poet Ennius listed him in the pantheon of twelve Roman gods. But it was over two hundred years after that before a temple was built in his honor (by Agrippa after a Roman naval victory).

Sailors reported seeing Neptune rising up from the water, which foamed around his great tail. He carried a trident with which—it was said—he could shatter rocks and call forth storms.

Neptunalia was celebrated on July 23rd.

Nereus (Greek): Son of Pontus, he was called "the Old Man of the Sea" and pre-dated the great Poseidon. Nereus was considered a trusty and gentle god. He and his wife, a daughter of Oceanus, had fifty daughters called the Nereids. One of his daughters married Poseidon. He is pictured as an old man with seaweed in his hair, living with his daughters in a cave at the bottom of the Aegean Sea.

Nethuns (Etruscan): This god of the water was closely associated with Neptune, and like him carried a trident.

Njord (Norse): One of the Vanir, the lesser gods who were closer to the people, Njord lived in Noatun, "the enclosure of ships." He was worshipped throughout Scandinavia and many places there still carry his name. He was god of ships as well as god of the sea.

Njord's ship, *Skioblaonir*, was large enough to hold all the gods and yet could be folded up and put in Njord's pocket. He was married by accident to Skadi, goddess of winter, before she married Odin. From an earlier marriage to his sister, Njord had a son and daughter, Frey and Freya.

So powerful was Njord that he continued ruling after the death of Odin. It is written in the thirteenth century Ynglinasaga that "in [Njord's] days good peace prevailed and there were such good crops of all kinds that the Swedes believe [he] had power over harvests..."

Basically Njord was considered a kind god. He controlled the wind, stilled the sea, and was involved in the lives of all sailors. Even into the late eighteenth century, Scandinavian fisherfolk still mentioned Njord in their prayers.

Nudd (British): Also known as Lludd, and by the Romans in Britain as Nodens or Nudons, this British river god guarded the headland of the River Severn. In the old Roman temple he was depicted as a beardless young man driving a chariot pulled by four horses and surrounded by tritons with horse forefeet.

Oannes (Sumerian): The Babylonian scholar-priest, Berossus, wrote about a race of monsters who emerged from the Persian Gulf led by a fish-man called Oannes. He had "a whole body... like that of a fish and had under a fish's head another head, also feet below, like those of a man joined to a fish's tail." According to Berossus, Oannes rose each morning from the sea and plunged in again at dusk.

Sometimes Oannes is pictured with a fish head for a cap or a fish-skin cloak that reached to his ankles.

Oannes was also called Lord of Wisdom, for it was he who taught humans civilization, giving the Sumerians the alphabet, science, art, house construction, laws, geometry, and knowledge of seeds and fruits. Because the Sumerians were transformed suddenly in 3500 BC from a hunting society to a civilized society, without any transitional period, there are people today who believe they were visited by fish-folk (aliens) from another planet!

In the Louvre is an eighth-century wall scene depicting Oannes as a merman.

Oceanus (Greek): A Titan who was considered Lord of the River Ocean, the great river that issued from the Greek underworld and encircled the flat earth. Oceanus fathered all the river gods on the female Titan, Tethys. His daughters were the nymphs known as Oceanids.

Olokun (Nigerian): God of Waters and the Deep, Olokun was the most worshipped god in the Benin kingdom. He is synonymous with the oceans of the earth. He provided humans with goods, health, women, and brings luck to ships and sailors.

In the Benin pantheon, Olokun represented purity, luck, happiness. His color was white, and he generally walked about on two enormous mudfish, carrying a lizard in each hand. Olokun was thought to live in a sea palace with his wives, who were the tributaries of the Ethiope River. His children were also thought to live in the palace, as well as Olokun's playmates, the mudfish.

Married women built mud altars in their homes in Olokun's

honor to insure fertility. Fresh river water, kept in mud pots, were placed on the altars daily.

O-Wata-Tsu-Mi (Japanese): The Old Man of the Tide is the greatest of Japanese sea gods. His messengers were the monster Wano, a shark, and a crocodile. He owned jewels that caused the ebb and flow of the tides.

Pikea (Polynesian): God of the sea monsters.

Pontus (Greek): God of the deep sea, Pontus was the son of Earth.

Poseidon (Greek): One of the three sons of Kronos—the other two being Zeus and Hades, Poseidon was ruler of the seas, rivers, streams, springs, and wells. Although his power was equal to Zeus's and he was sometimes called Zeus Elalios or Zeus Marine, Poseidon was still subject to Zeus and so was often in conflict with him.

Poseidon was pictured as huge, majestic, muscular, capable of great passion and rage. He was bearded with long, curling hair. His wealth came from all those treasures lost at sea.

Poseidon's symbols were the trident, the horse, and the bull. Horses were often sacrificed to him, especially in Thessaly, where it was believed Poseidon created the first horse by striking a rock with his trident. He is also credited with teaching men to domesticate the horse with the bridle. Other symbols of his rule include the tunnyfish and the dolphin.

Besides his residence on Mount Olympus, which he shared with the other gods, Poseidon had an undersea home near Aegea in Euboia where he slept on a golden couch. He emerged from the palace riding a golden chariot over the calmed waters. The chariot was drawn by golden-maned horses and accompanied by fish-men (tritons) blowing on conch-shell horns and sea animals.

In love with Amphitrite, whose netted hair was dressed with crab claws, Poseidon wooed her by sending the dolphin Delphinius as his messenger. Three children came from that union: son Triton and two daughters. Poseidon also sired a group of monsters, including Cyclops, as well as the winged horse Pegasus (from his love affair with Medusa), and the hero Theseus.

Poseidon's most celebrated temples were at the Isthmus of Corinth and on the headland at Sounion.

Proteus (Greek): This shapeshifting god slept with the seals in the likeness of a dirty, smelly old man. But if he were captured and held through his many shapeshifting changes—water, fire, serpent, lion—he would reward his captor by telling the truth about the future. In *The Odyssey*, Odysseus was able to capture Proteus.

Ryujin (Japanese): Also spelled Rinjin. The enormous-mouthed Japanese dragon king of the sea was also known as "Luminous Being." He controlled the tides with his magic jewels. He lived in Ryugu or Ryu Kyu, "Dragon's Court," a many-storied coral place where a single day is like a hundred years on land. Human fish are his courtiers and colorful dragons are his guards.

His daughter, Otohime, was called "The Immortal Bride."

Rongo (Hawaiian): One of the twin water gods of the Hawaiian people who, with his brother Tane, ran across the ocean bottom flying a kite.

Rongo-Mai (Polynesian): "Water Food," this is the god of whales, as well as comets.

Si-Raya (Malaysian): The spirit of the water from the low-water mark to mid-ocean. (*See* Mambang Tali Harus.)

Sobek (Egyptian): The crocodile god worshiped by sailors and fisher-folk. Crocodiles dedicated to him were kept in jeweled pools. His shrines can still be found in cities near water.

Sui-Tengu (Japanese): When the Shinto religion was joined to the Buddhist in Japan, the Indian god Varuna became associated with a local Osakan sea god, Sumiyoshi. Together they were given a new name: Sui-Tengu. Originally thought of as a sea god to whom sailors prayed to keep themselves safe from shipwreck, today Sui-Tengu is represented as a woman holding a child. That is because in 1185, the young emperor Antoku and his nurse were drowned in the Bay of Dan and the two subjects became confused.

Susanowo (Japanese): The storm god who is also the god of the oceans and the storms that rage over the waves.

Tagaloa (Samoa): Ocean god whose son was born in the shape of a bird. Tagaloa was the Samoan creator of earth, pushing up a rock for his bird son to land on.

Taidue (Aru Islands): The sea god to whom fishermen pray by dropping a gong over the side of the boat as a sacrifice for good fishing.

Tane (Hawaiian): *See* Rongo.

Tangaroa (Polynesian): God of the seas and patron of Polynesian fishermen, he was also called the Polynesian Poseidon and father of fish. Son of the earth goddess Papa, who swelled up with so much water when she was pregnant with him that when she expelled it all, it became the ocean. Because he was so big, Tangaroa breathed only twice in twenty-four hours, creating the tides. Sometimes he is portrayed as giving birth to all sea creatures, including mermen and mermaids. When he changes into a green lizard, fine weather is forecast.

In the Marquesas, Tangaroa was also known as Tanaoa and in Hawaii as Kanaloa. Some Polynesian and Micronesian sailors still place a piece of brain coral, representing the mind of the sea god, under the seat of their boats to keep them safe.

Tirnivan (Polynesian): Brother to Vatea, this lord of the fish was half man, half sprat.

Tlaloc (Mexican): God of the rains and waters, Tlaloc dwelled in the north, the place where the rains and streams were thought to begin. His cult goes right back to Toltec times. He is represented in drawings and carvings as having tusklike teeth and rings around his eyes. Sometimes a scroll emerges from his mouth instead of a tongue.

Tuna (Polynesian): The fish and vegetation god, Tuna was supposedly a man on the land and a fish in the sea. He lived in a submarine palace.

Varuna (Indian): According to Vedic myths, Varuna was once supreme ruler of all gods, but was demoted to a rain god called "the coverer" and then to the god of the sea. As such, he was called Vari-Lowa ("watery hair") and Yadapati ("king of water animals") and was thought to dwell at the springs of rivers, where all waters originate. In Gujarat he was known as "king of the waters who curbs the wicked, who made a road in the heavens to receive the rays of the sun."

A stern god, he rode on Makara—part elephant, crocodile, deer, and fish. The amazing Makara could fly through the sky, swim through the ocean, or race across land. Riding Makara, Varuna sat under a special umbrella made of a cobra's hood and no matter where he went, his clothing never got damp.

His two river-goddess wives were Jumna and Ganga. They lived apart from their husband who would visit them occasionally.

Vatea (Polynesian): Father of the gods and all humans, inventor of nets and fishing, Vatea was half human and half porpoise. Or half human and half shark. In Hawaii he was known as Wakea.

Viracocha (Peruvian): The white sea foam god who was one of the principle gods of Peru supposedly created the Incas. He was worshipped by the Peruvian Indians, who believed he rose up from Lake Titicaca bringing the arts and sciences, then disappeared, promising to return again.

Waruna (Balinese): Related to the Sanskrit Varuna, this is the God of oceans, rain, water, and the sea.

Wohhanda (Estonia): The Estonian river god, occasionally seen as a little man in blue and yellow stockings, he demanded sacrifices in the form of young children.

Wu (Dahoman/Benin): This sea god, also known as Hoo or Hwu, was so powerful that the priests used to beg his help in calming the waves by sacrificing an "ambassador" dressed in full splendor. The sacrifice would be thrown overboard far out in the ocean.

Yam Nahar (Ugaritic): God of both seas and rivers, Yam Nahar represented the hostile aspects of the waters such as storms, tidal waves, angry seas. In later years he was subdued by Baal, the god of fertility.

Zul (Finn-Ugric): Human-shaped though he lived under the water, this god was considered thoroughly evil.

Bibliography

GENERAL

Anson, Peter F. *Fisher Folk-Lore.* London: The Faith Press, 1965.

Aylesworth, Thomas G. *Werewolves and Other Monsters.* Reading, MA: Addison-Wesley, 1971.

Baker, Margaret. *Folklore of the Sea.* London: David & Charles, 1928.

Baring-Gould, S. *Curious Myths of the Middle Ages.* Boston: Robert Brothers, 1894.

Basset, Fletcher. *Legends and Superstitions of the Sea and Sailors.* Detroit: Singing Tree Press, 1971.

Beck, Horace. *Folklore of the Sea.* Mystic Seaport and Wesleyan University Press, 1973.

Thompson, C. J. S. *The Mystery and Lore of Monsters.* London: Williams & Norgate Ltd., 1930.

Campbell, Joseph. *The Mythic Image.* Princeton: Princeton University Press, 1974.

Carrington, R. *Mermaids and Mastodons.* New York: Holt, Rinehart and Winston, 1957.

Leach, Maria, et al. *Funk and Wagnall Standard Dictionary of Folklore, Mythology, and Legend.* New York: Funk and Wagnall, 1972.

Jastrow, Morris, Jr. *Handbook on the History of Religions.* Boston: Ginn and Co., 1902.

Lamont-Brown, Raymond. *Phantoms, Legends, Customs, and Superstitions of the Sea.* Glasgow: Brown, Son & Ferguson, 1972.

MacCulloch, Canon John Arnott. *The Childhood of Fiction: A Study of Folktales and Primitive Thought.* London: John Murray, 1905.

_____. *The Mythology of All Races.* 13 vols. Boston: Archeological Institute of America, 1927.

McHargue, Georgess. *The Impossible People.* New York: Holt, Rinehart and Winston, 1972.

New Larousse Encyclopedia of Mythology. New ed. London: Hamlyn Publishing Group, Ltd, 1968.

Robinson, H. S. and K. Wilson. *The Encyclopedia of Myths and Legends of All Nations.* New ed. London: Edmund Ward, 1962.

Sedgewick, Paulita. *Mythological Creatures.* New York: Holt, Rinehart and

Winston, 1974.

Thompson, C. J. S. *The Mystery and Lore of Monsters*. London: Williams & Norgate Ltd., 1930.

Thompson, Stith. *The Folktale*. New York: The Dryden Press, 1946.

White, T. H. *The Bestiary: A Book of Beasts*. New York: G. P. Putnam and Sons, 1954.

NORTHERN WATERS

Anderson, R. B. *Norse Mythology*. Chicago: S. C. Griggs & Co., 1979.

Buss, Reinhard J. *The Klabautermann of the Northern Seas*. Folklore Studies 25. Berkeley: University of California Press, 1973.

Davidson, H. R. Ellis. *Gods and Myths of Northern Europe*. London: Penguin, 1973.

Dumezil, Georges. *Gods of the Ancient Northmen*. Berkeley: University of California Press, 1973.

Grimm, Jacob. *Teutonic Mythology*. Vol 1. London: W. Swan Connenchen and Allen, 1880.

Grimm, Jacob and Wilhelm. *German Sagas*. Vol. 11, number 55. 1816/1818.

Guerber, H. A. *Myths of Northern Lands*. New York: American Book Co., 1895.

Haupt, Karl. *The Waternixen, the Wasserman and His Wife*. Leipzeig: Verlag von Wilhelm Engelmann, 1862.

Hopp, Zinken. *Norwegian Folklore Simplified*. Bergen: John Griegs Forlag, 1961.

Kearny, Charles Francis. *Outlines of Primitive Beliefs Among the Indo-European Races*. New York: Charles Scribner's Sons, 1882.

Mortenson, Karl. *Norse Mythology*. New York: Thomas Y. Crowell, 1913.

Saussaye, P. D. Cahntepie de la. *The Religion of the Teutons*. Boston: Ginn and Co., 1902.

Simpson, Jacqueline. *Icelandic Folktales and Legends*. Berkeley: University of California Press, 1972.

Stern, Herbert I. *The Gods of Our Fathers*. New York: Harper and Brothers, 1898.

Thorpe, Benjamin. *Northern Mythology*. London: Edward Lumley, 1852.

West, John F. *Faroese Folk-Tales & Legends*. Lerwick, Shetland: Shetland Publishing Company, 1980.

www.pitt.edu/~dash/water.html Folklore and Mythological Electronic Texts.

RUSSIA AND THE SLAVIC COUNTRIES

Alexander, Alex E. *Russian Folklore.* Belmont, MA: Norland Publishing Co., 1975.

Guterman, Norburt. *Russian Fairy Tales.* New York: Pantheon Books, 1945.

Kavcic, Vladimir. *The Golden Bird.* New York: World Publishing and Co., 1895.

Quinn, Zdenka and John Paul. *Folktales of Bohemia.* Philadelphia: Macrae Smith, 1971.

Ralston, W. R. S. *Russian Folktales.* New York: Lowell, Adam, Wesson & Co., n.d.

BRITISH ISLES

Anson, Peter. *Fisher Folk-lore.* London: The Faith Press, 1965.

Bord, Janet and Colin. *Sacred Waters: Holy Wells and Water Lore in Britain and Ireland.* London: Collins Publishing Group, 1986.

Briggs, Katherine M. *The Anatomy of Puck.* London: Routledge and Kegan Paul Ltd., 1959.

_____. *British Folk-Tales and Legends: A Sampler.* London: Routledge and Kegan Paul Ltd., 1977.

_____. *A Dictionary of British Folk-Tales in the English Language.* 4 vols. London: Routledge and Kegan Paul, 1970–77.

_____. *Fairies in English Tradition and Literature.* Chicago: University of Chicago Press, 1967.

Campbell, Joseph. *The Mask of God: Creative Mythology.* New York: Viking Compass Books, 1968.

"Celtic Review." Vols. 2 and 3. David Nutt, n.d.

Dorson, Richard M. *Peasant Customs and Savage Myths.* Vol. 2. London: Routledge & Kegan Paul Ltd., 1968.

Grierson, Elizabeth W. *The Scottish Fairy Book.* London: Fisher Unwin, n.d.

Henderson, George. *The Celtic Dragon Myth.* Edinburgh: John Grant, 1911.

Hull, Eleanor. *The Cuchullin Saga in Irish Literature.* London: David Nutt, 1898.

Hyde, Douglas. *A Literary History of Ireland.* London: Fisher Unwin, 1901.

Johnson, W. Branch. *Folktales of Brittany.* London: Methuen & Co. Ltd., 1927.

Keightly, Thomas. *The Fairy Mythology.* London: H. G. Bohn, 1850.

Kennedy, Patrick. *Legendary Fictions of the Irish Celts.* London: Macmillan and Co., 1866.

Killip, Margaret. *The Folklore of the Isle of Man.* London: B. T. Batsford Ltd., 1975.

Lawson, John Cuthbert. *Modern Greek Folklore and Ancient Greek Religion.* Cambridge: Cambridge University Press, 1910.

Moray, Ann. *A Fair Stream of Silver.* New York: Morrow, 1965.

Rhys, John. *Celtic Folklore: Welsh and Manx.* Vol. 2. Oxford: The Clarendon Press, 1901.

Robertson, E. Macdonald. *Selected Highland Folktales.* London: Oliver & Boyd, 1961.

Rolleston, T. W. *Myths and Legends of the Celtic Race.* London: George C. Harrap & Co., 1912.

Saul, George Brandon. *The Shadow of the Three Queens: A Handbook Introduction to the Traditional Irish literature and Its Backgrounds.* Harrison, PA: The Stackpole Co., 1953.

Spence, Lewis. *The Minor Traditions of British Mythology.* London: Rider, 1948.

Squire, Charles. *Celtic Myth and Legend, Poetry and Romance.* Hollywood: Newcastle Publishing Co., 1975.

Teit, J. A. "Water Beings in Shetlandic Folk-Lore as Remembered by Shetlanders in British Columbia." *Journal of American Folk-Lore.* Ed. Franz Boas. American Folklore Society, 1919.

Williamson, Duncan. *Tales of the Sea People.* Northampton, MA., Interlink Publishing, 1992.

Wimberly, H. *Folklore in English and Scottish Ballads.* Chicago: University of Chicago Press, 1928.

Yeats, William Butler. *Irish Fairy and Folktales.* New York: Grosset and Dunlap, 1974.

SOUTHERN EUROPE

Abbot, G. F. *Macedonian Folklore.* Cambridge: The University Press, 1903.

Aeschylus. *Seven Against Thebes.* Trans. D. Fitts and R. Fitzgerald. The Complete Greek Tragedy Series. Chicago: University of Chicago Press, 1957.

Argenti, Philip and H. J. Rose. *The Folklore of Chios.* Cambridge: The University Press, 1949.

Aristophanes. *The Knights.* Trans. D. Fitts and R. Fitzgerald. The

Complete Greek Tragedy Series. Chicago: University of Chicago Press, 1957.

Bulfinch, Thomas. *The Age of Fable*. New York: Doubleday, 1968.

Campbell, Joseph. *The Hero with a Thousand Faces*. Princeton: Bollingen Press, 1949.

_____. *The Mask of God: Occidental Mythology*. New York: Viking Press, 1962.

Graves, Robert. *The Greek Myths*. New York: Penguin Books, 1955.

Guthrie, W. K. C. *The Greeks and Their Gods*. Boston: Beacon Press, 1955.

Hamilton, Edith. *Mythology*. New York: Mentor Books, 1953.

_____. *Mythology: Timeless Tales of Gods and Heroes*. New York: New American Library, 1940.

Harding, Caroline and Samuel. *Greek Gods: Heroes and Men*. Chicago: Scott, Foresman & Co., 1909.

Harvey, Sir Paul. *The Oxford Companion to Classical Literature*. Oxford: Clarendon Press, 1937.

Homer. *The Odyssey*. Trans. Robert Fitzgerald. Garden City, NY: Doubleday and Co., n.d.

Johnson, W. Branch. *Folktales of Brittany*. London: Methuen & Co. Ltd., 1927.

Lawson, John Cuthbert. Modern Greek Folklore and Ancient Greek Religions. Cambridge: Cambridge University Press, 1910.

Pliny. *Natural History of Plinius Secundus*. Trans. Philemon Holland.

Reinhold, Meyer. *Classics: Greek and Roman*. Great Neck, NY: Barron's Educational Series, Inc., 1946.

Robinson, H. S. and Wilson K. *The Encyclopedia of Myths and Legends of All Nations*. 2nd ed. London: Edmund Ward, 1962.

Seyfert, Oskar. *Dictionary of Classical Antiquities*. New York: Meridan Books, 1891.

Sophocles. *Oedipus at Colonnus*. Trans. D. Fitts and R. Fitzgerald. The Complete Greek Tragedy Series. Chicago: University of Chicago Press, 1957.

Tripp, Edward. *The Meridan Handbook of Classical Mythology*. New York: New American Library, 1970.

ASIA

Christie, Anthony. *Chinese Mythology*. London: Paul Hamlyn, 1968.

Dorson, Richard M. *Folk Legends of Japan*. Rutland, VT: Charles E. Tuttle Co., 1962.

_____. *Studies in Japanese Folklore.* Bloomington: Indiana University Press, 1963.

Dubose, Rev. Hampden C. *The Dragon, Image and Demon, or the Three Religions of China.* London: S. W. Partridge & Co., 1886.

Eberhard, Wolfram. *Folktales of China.* Rev. ed. Chicago: University of Chicago, 1965.

Hackin, J. *Asiatic Mythology.* New York: Crescent Books, n.d.

Hopkins, Edward Washburn. *The Religion of India.* Boston: Ginn and Co., 1895.

Junne, I. K. *Floating Clouds, Floating Dreams: Favorite Asian Folktales.* New York: Doubleday & Company, Inc., 1974

Kearny, Charles Francis. *Outlines of Primitive Belief among the Indo-European Races.* New York: Charles Scribner's Sons & David Nutt, 1897.

Keith, A. B. *Religion and Philosophy of the Vedas and Upanishads.* Westport, CT: Greenwood Press, n.d.

Mackenzie, Donald A. *China and Japan.* Myths and Legends Series. New York: Avenal Books, 1985.

O'Neill, John. *The Night of the Gods.* Vol. 2. London: Harrison & Sons & David Nutt, 1897.

Philip, Neil. *The Spring of Butterflies and Other Folktales of China's Minority Peoples.* Trans. He Liyi. New York: Lothrop, Lee & Shepard Books, 1986.

Pyle, Katharine. *Wonder Tales from Many Lands.* London: George G. Harrap & Company Ltd., 1920.

Roberts, Moss, ed and trans. *Chinese Fairy Tales and Fantasies.* New York: Pantheon Books, 1979.

Tyler, Royall. *Japanese Tales.* New York: Pantheon Books, 1987.

MIDDLE EAST

Al-Shahi, Ahmed and F. C. T. Moore. *Wisdom from the Nile.* Oxford: Clarendon Press, 1978.

Burton, Richard F., ed and trans. *The Book of the Thousand Nights and a Night.* Vol. 9. Printed by the Burton Club for private subscribers, n.d.

Campbell, Joseph. *The Mask of God: Oriental Mythology.* New York: Viking Press, 1962.

Frankfort, Henri, et al. *Before Philosophy.* New York: Penguin Books, 1952.

_____. *The Birth of Civilization in the Near East.* Bloomington: Indiana

University Press, 1954.

_____. *The Intellectual Adventure of Ancient Man.* Chicago: University of Chicago Press, 1946.

Heidl, Alexander. *The Babylonian Genesis: The Story of the Creation.* 2nd ed. Chicago: University of Chicago Press, 1954.

_____. *The Gilgamesh Epic and Old Testament Parallels.* Chicago: University of Chicago Press, 1954.

Jastrow, Morris Jr. *The Religion of Babylonia and Assyria.* Boston: Athenaeum Press, 1898.

King, L. W., ed. *Enuma Elish: The Seven Tablets of Creation.* London: Luzac & Co., 1902.

Kirk, G. S. *Myth: Its Function and Meaning in Ancient and Other Cultures.* Berkeley: University of California Press, 1970.

Kramer, S. N. *Sumerian Mythology.* Philadelphia: American Philosophical Society, 1944.

Legey, Francoise. *The Folklore of Morocco.* London: George Allen & Unwin Ltd, 1926.

Madrus, Dr. J. C. *Le Livre des Mille Nuits et Une Nuit.* Vol. 9. Bruxelles: Edition La Boetie, 1899.

Pritchard, J. B., ed. *The American Near East.* Princeton: Princeton University Press, 1958.

AFRICA

Dorson, Richard M. *African Folklore.* Bloomington: Indiana University Press, 1972.

Knappert, Jan. *African Mythology: An Encyclopedia of Myth and Legend.* London: Diamond Books, 1995.

PACIFIC ISLANDS

Knappert, Jan. *Pacific Mythology: An Encyclopedia of Myth and Legend.* London: Diamond Books, 1995.

Smith, W. Ramsay. *Myths and Legends of the Australian Aboriginals.* London: George G. Harrap & Company Ltd., 1930.

NEW WORLD

Burland, C., Nicholson, I., and Osborne, H. *Mythology of the Americas.* London: Hamyn, 1970.

Clark, Ella E. *Indian Legends of the Pacific Northwest.* Berkeley: University of California Press, 1963.

Courlander, Harold. *A Treasury of Afro-American Folklore.* New York: Crown Publishers, Inc., 1976.

_____. *The Drum and the Hoe: Life and Lore of the Haitian People.* Berkeley: University of California Press, 1960.

Erdoes, Richard, and Alfonso Ortiz. *American Indian Myths and Legends.* New York: Pantheon Books, 1984.

Gifford, Douglas. *Warriors, Gods, and Spirits from Central and South American Mythology.* Glasgow: Eurobooks Ltd., 1983

Rasmussen, Knut. *Eskimo Folktales.* Copenhagen: Gyldendal, 1921.

Slater, Candace. *Dance of the Dolphin: Transformation and Disenchantment in the Amazonian Imagination.* Chicago: University of Chicago Press, 1994.

Spence, Lewis. *North American Indians' Myths and Legends.* London: George G. Harrap & Company Ltd., 1994.